A Whispered Curse: The Shadows of Oak Hollow

By Brandy Nacole

A Whispered Curse: The Shadows of Oak Hollow

Cover Art by Brandy Nacole
Published by Brandy Nacole, LLC
Copyright@2025 Brandy Nacole, LLC

All rights reserved.

No part of this book may be reproduced or transmitted in any form or by any means, electronic or mechanical, including photocopying, recording or by any information storage and retrieval system, without written permission from the publisher.

The unauthorized reproduction or distribution of copyrighted work is illegal. Criminal copyright infringement, including infringement without monetary gain, is investigated by the FBI and is punishable by fines and federal imprisonment.

This is a work of fiction. All characters and situations appearing in this work are fictitious. Any resemblance to real persons, living or dead, or personal situations is purely coincidental.

Chapter One	11
Chapter Two	18
Chapter Three	32
Chapter Four	42
Chapter Five	51
Chapter Six	58
Chapter Seven	66
Chapter Eight	74
Chapter Nine	80
Chapter Ten	87
Chapter Eleven	94
Chapter Twelve	99
Chapter Thirteen	107
Chapter Fourteen	117
Chapter Fifteen	122
Chapter Sixteen	126
Chapter Seventeen	134
Chapter Eighteen	143
Chapter Nineteen	149
Chapter Twenty	151
Chapter Twenty-One	160
Chapter Twenty-Two	166
Chapter Twenty-Four	172
Chapter Twenty-Five	179
Chapter Twenty-Six	181

One Year Later... 186
About the Author..191
Other Books by Brandy..192

For those who chase the unknown, even when it whispers back.

Some believe that madness can ignite the most noble of intentions. However, for my family, this madness became a catalyst for destruction, unraveling the very fabric of our lives and leading us down a path of chaos and despair. What began as well-meaning impulses quickly spiraled out of control, leaving us grappling with the consequences of our actions and the painful aftermath of our choices.

Chapter One

"Amara."

I blinked away the tears burning my eyes and turned to Dad. I had to be strong. I had to hold onto the pain for just a little longer. "Yes?"

"Which color should I wear?" He held up two shirts he had chosen for the ceremony. One was solid black with silver snap buttons, while the other was dark blue, featuring the same silver snap buttons. He likely bought them at the hardware store for today. Otherwise, he would have been wearing his solid grey t-shirt and jeans.

"Blue. Mom would love it." She preferred not to wear black for funerals, believing it was too morbid. Instead, she thought white was more appropriate for celebrating life.

It was why I was wearing the floral green dress she bought for me last year. "We should get going."

Dad nodded and held out his arm for me to take. My smile was weak as I did. I shouldn't be here. I shouldn't be witnessing the sorrow in Dad's eyes or hiding mine as it eats me alive. This was all her fault. If she had stopped chasing lies like I begged her to do, she'd be here. Her madness led to our family's destruction.

The drive across town was silent. The dim buildings passed with a familiarity that made me numb to the thrumming pain inside.

Dad reached across the space between us and took my hand. "You need to let go of that hate. It will eat at you, the same as the stories ate at her."

I don't know if that will ever be possible. The pain and anger were too great. I do my best for my dad and squeeze his hand. "I know, Dad."

The funeral was a somber gathering, resonating with the sound of muffled sobs and softly spoken tributes to my mother from her friends and family. As I looked around the room, I felt a wave of bitterness wash over me. These were the very people who I believed had abandoned her long ago, yet here they were, draped in black and sharing tender memories. It made my stomach churn to listen to their heartfelt recollections. They spoke lovingly of a woman I hardly knew. It was a version of my mother that felt foreign to me.

When the time came for me to speak, my throat tightened, and tears streamed down my face as I instinctively buried my head in my hands. I sobbed unabashedly, overwhelmed by emotion and desperate to avoid the podium. It wasn't that I was unwilling to share my thoughts about her; rather, I feared what might tumble out if I allowed myself to speak. The anger I harbored toward her felt too raw, too private to expose to an audience. I could already imagine the whispers and judgment from those who had no understanding of my history with her. They were never there to witness the chaos.

Dad squeezed my hand, his grip firm and reassuring. He wore an expression of quiet resignation, perhaps aware of the conflicting emotions that churned beneath the surface, yet grateful that I was keeping my composure. He didn't attempt to speak on her behalf, either. Dad had never been one to display his emotions openly. His stoicism was a shield, a silent pact to keep our family's struggles in the dark where no one could judge us. In this moment, I recognized the weight of our shared grief, tempered by the unspoken truths we each carried alone.

After we laid Mom to rest, the community center filled with familiar faces, all gathered for what should have been a moment of remembrance and comfort. Yet, amidst the somber occasion, I felt a strange disconnect. It was peculiar to witness so many people come together for her after all the whispered judgments I had witnessed as a child. I could still hear the echoes of the snide comments, such as "Crazy Esme," that crept in hushed tones when she was within earshot. Their laughter would trail behind her like a shadow.

Mom had always been fervently devoted to her interests, pouring her heart and soul into her passions. However, this passion often came with an unpredictability that unsettled those around her, leading to an uneasy community dynamic. They never hesitated to let her know how they felt, their uncomfortable glances and snickers fueling her desire to prove them wrong.

As I stood in the corner of the room, the noise of polite chatter and muffled weeping washed over me, but I felt isolated. My heart ached not only for her loss but for the life that now beckoned me beyond this place. I'd built a life for myself. A life far removed from the tales and family folklore that had woven a complicated web around my childhood. I wanted to run out the doors and go to the comforts I had away from the small-town whispers and the weight of expectation. All I sought was to be me, unburdened and free.

"Hey."

Lost in my thoughts, I suddenly jolted at the sound of a familiar voice. When I turned to see who it was, a grin spread across my face, and I rushed into his warm embrace. "Oh my god, Laken! I've missed you so much."

As he wrapped his arms around me, I felt a wave of comfort wash over me, just like old times. After a moment, he pulled back to meet my gaze, his expression genuine. "Unlike the rest of these idiots, I'm really sorry to hear about your mom."

His words brought a soft smile to my lips. Laken had always shared my disdain for this town. "Thanks. It was a real shock," I admitted, pausing to consider my own words. "Or maybe it wasn't."

His brow arched in intrigue, a mixture of surprise and understanding. "So, you're still mad at her, then." The way he said it was more of an observation than a question, as if he had already pieced together the remnants of my tangled feelings.

"Even in death," I said, unguarded and resolute. The truth hung in the air between us. It was as undeniable as the weight of grief that settled in my chest. "I love her and will miss her deeply, but everything that happened was her fault."

A playful shove came from my left, breaking through the somber mood. I turned to see a familiar face, and a rush of warmth surged through me as a genuine smile spread across my face. "No freaking way! Cori! I thought you had bailed on this place for good."

Cori's embrace enveloped me, her energy as familiar and comforting as Laken's. No matter how much time passed, the bond we shared felt unbreakable. "I did take off for a while," she said, her eyes sparkling with mischief, "but you know how it is. Eventually, I got sucked back into the hometown cliché. It's like a gravitational pull!"

I couldn't help but laugh, my mood brightening. There were times when I missed the small town we grew up in, despite its many flaws. Memories swirled in my mind, some sweet but many tinged with pain. It was a double-edged sword. "Well, as long as you're genuinely happy to be back, that's all that matters," I replied, sincerity lacing my words.

At that moment, Laken pulled a crumpled twenty-dollar bill from his pocket, waving it around like a trophy. He approached Cori, handing it to her with a teasing grin plastered on his face. "Here you go!"

"Thanks!" she exclaimed, her delight lighting up her features.

I couldn't help but shake my head in disbelief. "Are you two seriously still at it?" I asked, amusement creeping into my voice as I recalled all the ridiculous wagers they had made over the years, often at others' expense. In middle school, it had been innocent dares and candy. By high school, the stakes had elevated to cash, and their little game had taken on a life of its own.

"Of course!" Laken replied with a nonchalant shrug, as if it were the most normal thing in the world.

"What did you bet on this time?" I asked, my gut tightening with apprehension as I noticed the knowing look exchanged between them. I had a sinking feeling I already knew the answer.

Cori leaned in, her voice dropping to a conspiratorial whisper. "If you were still mad at your mom or not."

I wasn't surprised. Before I left, the small community bore witness to the painful transformation that had overtaken my mother. They were all too familiar with the fallout of our relationship and the resentment that had begun to fester between us like a wound that refused to heal. It was evident to everyone that my departure was an inevitable choice.

"Well, congratulations, Cori," I said, trying to mask my swirling emotions. As the weight of the day pressed down on me, I sank into the chair at the table next to us, feeling utterly drained. Cori and Laken slid into seats across from me, their expressions a mix of happiness and concern. "You know, I do love her," I continued, my voice barely above a whisper. "I just… I couldn't understand her actions, and that lack of understanding turned into anger that I didn't know how to express."

Once again, I noticed Cori and Laken exchanging glances, a silent conversation passing between them that I wasn't part of. I wasn't naïve. I could tell they had been discussing something significant, something they were hesitant to share with me. Their eyes held a weight of unspoken thoughts, and I felt the tension thickening in the air.

I braced myself, ready to face whatever they had to say. "Just tell me," I urged.

"It's about your mother," Laken began, his voice laced with uncertainty. I had anticipated as much.

Cori leaned forward, her palms pressed firmly against the table as if steeling herself for impact. "We don't think she was completely wrong," she admitted.

My jaw dropped in disbelief. "You can't be serious."

Laken swallowed hard, his eyes darting away from mine. "I've been helping your mom for the last two years."

"Helping her?" I shot back, my tone sharper than I intended, and I could see Cori flinch at my words. "Helping her how?"

Laken fidgeted with his hands, avoiding my gaze. "It started with her just needing some muscle. She was getting older, you know? She needed someone to help carry her stuff in the woods."

A harsh laugh escaped me, tinged with disbelief. "Are you seriously telling me you camped out in the woods with my mother for weeks? The same woman you used to call insane after one of our many fights. That woman."

He nodded.

"Unbelievable." I turned to Cori, seeking some clarity. "What about you? Were you involved too?"

Cori shook her head. "Your mom hired Laken, but when I offered to come along, she said no. She insisted it was too dangerous."

It was what Mom always said, even when I was a kid. Yet, every time she came back unharmed. That was because the legend wasn't true and she'd spent her whole life chasing a damn shadow.

I guess bought help was the exception to the rule. Laken refuses to look at me when I turn my attention back to him. "Hey." I slap my hand on the table in front of him. The pop isn't loud, but it catches his attention. "When did you start believing her?"

"After our second trip. I don't want to dive into it here, but you have to believe me, Amara. Something truly strange happened out there. I swear to you, it did." As he spoke, the sincerity in his eyes was palpable, a depth of conviction that reminded me of the look my mother often wore. She had held that same expression for most of my life, an aching blend of hope and sorrow. She clung to the belief in something that, in my eyes, had always been a façade.

The weight of this conversation settled uncomfortably between us, and I felt no urge to continue. Rising to my feet, I brushed a few strands of hair behind my ear and said, "It was good seeing you both, but I really need to track down my father."

Laken instinctively reached out, his hand stretching toward mine. Just then, Cori gripped his arm firmly, her expression sharp enough to cut through any lingering warmth in the air. He glanced back at her, seeking her approval or perhaps understanding, but she simply met his gaze with a determined glare. "Now is not the time, Laken. We should let Amara focus on the funeral. Perhaps, we can all get together before she leaves town," she said, her tone accepting no argument.

I offered them both a nod and a faint smile, masking the swirl of emotions within me. "We should," I agreed, even though my heart was heavy with the knowledge that as much as I missed the two of them, that was one meeting I would be certain to avoid.

Chapter Two

Two days had passed since my mother's funeral, and I was beyond ready to leave this place. The only thing stopping me was my father. I placed my cellular dynamics textbook on the table and set off for the kitchen. While here, I'd been taking the quiet opportunity to study, but my heart wasn't in it. I hated the quiet hum that filled the room, even though Dad and I occupied it. We both had so much to say, but neither of us was willing to utter the words.

I found Dad in the kitchen, soaking Mom's air plants. "I remember when we started getting those for her." A genuine smile tilted my lips and warmed my cheeks. "I thought it was the most ridiculous thing."

A soft smile also brightened his face. "I remember. You killed the first two we had because plants need water."

I'd never seen a plant rot so fast. "While it wasn't the best plant for me, it was definitely the best one for her." Mom loved plants but was never home long enough to keep them alive. Air plants were made for people like her.

"It's always been that way with you two," Dad remarked as he hung the plants back up.

I grabbed two coffee mugs and started the kettle. I could feel the conversation that had been brewing for days was about to explode. The day before I left, no doubt.

"What do you mean?"

Dad turned to face me and leaned back against the wall with his arms crossed. He'd been doing that a lot the past few days—crossing his arms. It's as if he were having to hold himself together. "The way you two viewed life. It's why you ran away from us. You couldn't stand the way your mother was so passionate about her work. It killed you and your beliefs to watch her."

Heat rushed up my body as I held back the anger threatening to unleash on my father. He was the one person who always seemed to be in my corner, but was now taking a defensive turn on me. He never did that when she was alive, so why now, when she's gone? "I left for a lot of reasons, including finding the science that would help her realize she was chasing shadows and stories."

Dad let out a harsh laugh. "How can you say that after what happened to her?"

The kettle began to whistle, and I let it go a second longer than necessary. On some small level, it was expressing my deep disappointment and anger that he was doing this. "That's the thing, we don't know what happened. She decided to go alone that day. For all we know, she fell."

"You're right. We don't know what happened, but the evidence is contradictory." He took the mug of tea I offered him and set it on the counter. I gently stir mine as I added too much water in my haste to make it.

As I do, I weigh my options. I could continue arguing with him and making this situation worse, which was what I wanted to do. Every fiber of my being wanted to defend why I left and the purpose behind my studies. Still, looking at him now, I also know he is a man in mourning. He's going to protect his wife's honor and everything she believed, as it's what ultimately took her from him.

Laying my spoon down, I reached across the counter and placed my hand on his. "I don't want to fight. No matter what happened, we lost an amazing woman. Let's not forget that."

He turned his hand over and squeezed my hand. "You're right. She was an amazing woman." His eyes got watery, and he quickly pulled away to wipe away the evidence.

Taking a drink of my tea, I turned away to give him a moment to collect himself. Dad never was one to show his emotions. I also took the time to conceal my feelings. It frustrated me to no end that everyone around here thinks I left to spite my mother. That was never my intention. I wanted to help her and show her that the life she was chasing was nothing but a fantasy. I wanted her to snap into a reality that was livable, not obsessive and false.

"There's something else I've been meaning to talk to you about." Dad collected himself and was now back in control. "Your mother left all her research material to you, but considering your stance on the matter, I'd like to give it all to Laken Clarke."

That came as a surprise. The last thing I would have expected my mother to leave me was her precious research. I figured she'd think I would tear it apart, which was probably why my father wanted to give it away.

A part of me wanted to say no. It was my mother's life's work. It would be like giving away her wedding ring, which she didn't have because she pawned it to buy new equipment and could never get it back. Still, it was precious to her. Letting it go seemed wrong, but there was no mistaking I didn't want it either.

"That's fine," I remarked offhandedly, though as I said it, it felt like a betrayal.

"I figured you'd say that, which is why I told him he could come by today and get it all," he replied, his tone so unnervingly casual I wanted to scream.

The news was just as shocking as finding out Mom would leave me her research. What would he have done if I said I wanted it?

Before I can say more, the doorbell rings. I glance around the corner to see Laken standing at the door. It was like fate brought him at the right moment to deliver the final blow.

Dad stands from his perch at the bar. "Speak of the devil." I'd say so. "Can you let Laken in? I'll go start gathering the boxes."

Boxes?

Still feeling a bit shocked, I let my body take control and move towards the door. It felt as though this moment was foreign to me, and my body didn't know how to react. Am I ready to let it all go?

I felt the smile as I opened the door, but I didn't connect with it. It's automatic. As is my greeting. "Oh, hey Laken."

He seemed as surprised to see me. "Oh, hey, Amara. I figured you already went back to school."

Did everyone think so poorly of me? "I stayed behind to help Dad sort out things. Ya know, keep him company."

"That's good," he says, while digging his hands deeper in his pockets.

It took a full breath or two before my brain processed that I needed to let him in. Or was it that unsettled part of me still refusing to accept what was about to happen? "Come in. Dad just said he was expecting you."

Laken stepped inside but made no effort to relax. He radiated an unmistakable nervousness. I couldn't quite grasp why my presence seemed to unsettle him. What was it about me that made him so uneasy?

"Would you like some tea?" I asked, hoping to break the tension. It didn't. He fidgeted more.

"No, thank you."

I could hear Dad rummaging around in the back room where Mom kept all her stuff. I almost made a break to go help him when Laken cleared his throat, and we made eye contact. I could tell he wanted to say something, but was too afraid to say it.

I could help with that. "What's on your mind?"

"It's nothing." He shrugged and looked away, his movements familiar. It's how he acted when we dated. Casual, but full of so much left unsaid.

And just like then, I called his bluff. "I promise, whatever it is, you can tell me. Dad just threw some pretty harsh blows, and I took them."

He paused, unsure. I expected it. I also knew he would cave and tell me what was on his mind. "It's just something you said at your mother's funeral. I wanted you to know that she wasn't crazy. What happened out there that day was real, and I wish you'd give me the chance to prove it to you."

This I didn't expect. Laken, of all people, knew how I felt about what happened to my mother. "There's nothing to prove. Besides, I have to get back and finish my FINAL." Even if I had nothing to get back to, I wouldn't stay around to witness more of what I knew was foolish nonsense.

"Amara, I really think—"

"Here we are." Dad stormed into the room with a heavy box in hand. "You can take this one, and I'll go get the rest."

Rather than stay with Laken and continue this awkward conversation, I followed Dad to the back room. He went to pick up one of the larger boxes, but paused. There's a hitch in his breath as he turned back to face me. "No matter what that boy says, I don't want you to cave to his suggestions. He already hurt you once. I won't see it happen again."

A soft smile touched my lips. "Dad, that was years ago." The thought of Laken no longer brings the deep, dreaded pain I'd once felt before going to college. He may have broken my heart, but I also like to think he made me stronger.

"Still, I don't trust him when it comes to your heart. As trivial as that sounds, there's more at stake regarding your feelings than young love." His rough, callous fingers cupped my face with affection.

I leaned into his love. "I know." Laken trying to convince me that my mom was right would dredge up more pain than just a little love affair. My dad didn't want me to face that any more than I already was.

We finished helping Laken load the boxes into his car. A part of me hated how easily I was letting go of Mom's research. It was such a big part of her life. But as Laken slammed the trunk shut, I flinched away, knowing this was for the best. I wouldn't have faith in it like she did. I'm more skeptic than believer.

"Thanks again, Mr. Hayes." He turned to me with an easy smile crossing his lips. "Stay safe, Amara." He twirled his keys as he walked around the car to the driver's side. He stopped before getting into the car and looked over the roof at me. "Think about what I said. You deserve the truth, even if it's hard to hear." Then, he was gone.

Dad shook his head as he turned for the house, muttering under his breath. I stood there frozen, looking after Laken with hesitation. He wasn't wrong. I did deserve the truth, but the truth didn't lie in the woods. It was back at my lab, where I would one day be able to prove this whole town wrong. It all came down to the science.

Still, as his taillights faded, the heaviness of my leaving became even heavier. Was I leaving, or was I running away?

The car's engine rumbled, its low hum almost drowned out by the soft rustling of the wind through the trees. I sat at the stop sign, staring at the rearview mirror. The fading outline of my hometown, where the last few houses clustered like memories clung to the edge of the world, filled the reflection. The streetlights ahead were flickering off one by one, a quiet signal that morning was beginning to settle over the town.

A knot formed in my stomach. *Are you leaving or running away?*

I glanced at the side mirror and caught a glimpse of the breathtaking rising sun as it bathed the streets in golden hues. My dad's truck had just turned the corner, leaving me alone at the edge of town. He was heading back to work, returning to his routine. It felt like the world was gently pushing me forward, yet another force kept me tethered here.

We had hugged as we said our goodbyes. Dad's arms held me tightly, a shield against the impending distance. It was a comfort I cherished. When we finally pulled apart, the reality of our goodbye hit me like a wave.

"I'll visit during the holidays, I promise," he said, his voice steady, but I caught a hint of vulnerability in his eyes that mirrored my own. I nodded, trying to smile through the tightness in my throat, but inside, I felt an unsettling mix of hope and dread.

Returning to university was the logical path; it was what I had worked so hard for. Yet, as I took those first steps away from him, I couldn't shake the gnawing feeling that I was leaving something bigger behind.

I had convinced myself that this was the right decision, that I had made peace with it. But sitting there in the car with the engine running, I couldn't shake the feeling that something was missing. Or maybe it was more than just something. It was a gnawing sensation in the pit of my stomach, an emptiness that had only deepened in the last few days.

Laken's words echoed in my mind.

"You can't just leave. Not yet."

I'd laughed it off when he said it, told him that I needed a fresh start, that there was nothing left for me here. But now, in the car's silence, it felt like a lie. I wasn't running toward anything. I was running away. From what, though? From the truth?

What truth?

His voice was so confident that it unsettled me. The notion that something was buried beneath the surface—something I didn't know but needed to—gnawed at me like a forgotten dream trying to resurface. The way he looked at me when he said it made me feel like I was the only one capable of unraveling whatever had been hidden from me.

"You deserve the truth, even if it's hard to hear."

I squeezed my eyes shut, willing myself to focus. I could still hear Laken's voice, clear and steady. It was as if he were sitting beside me, urging me to turn back. To stay and dig into whatever was buried here.

I pushed open the car door and stepped out, the cold bite of the morning air wrapping around me. The sky had already lightened, but I could still make out the dim lights of the town behind me. My hands shoved into my jacket pockets as I started to pace slowly, my shoes crunching the gravel underfoot.

What if Laken was right? What if I was running away from something I shouldn't?

The truth. That's what it all came down to. I wanted to prove this town wrong and show them the real pain behind my mother's death. The pain of her dying from their lies and fears.

So much was left unsaid between my dad and me about what happened with Mom. Why did he let her believe the impossible? Why did he never stop her?

I tried to picture my dad's face when I left. When I said goodbye, I didn't really look at him. I hadn't let myself linger, knowing it would be the last time for who knows how long. The distance between us had always been there, like a wall I couldn't climb or tear down. Did he not want me near Laken or just not here at all?

The quiet of the morning seemed to press in on me, each breath I took feeling heavier than the last. I stopped walking, my feet planted firmly on the gravel road, and let myself think for a moment. What was I so afraid of?

I heard the faint hum of an engine. It was like an anchor pulling me in, telling me I could still turn back if I wanted to. But how could I face it all? How could I ask about all the things I'd avoided? I wasn't sure I could bear what I might find.

Laken had said I deserved the truth. He did too.

Shaking my head, I tried to clear the thoughts swirling in my mind. The cold wind stung my face, but it did nothing to clear the confusion. A voice inside whispered that I had to know. I had to ask the questions. If not now, then when? If not me, who?

Laken's voice stayed with me, unraveling all the uncertainty. It was time to face it all.

I stepped away from the car while pulling out my phone. I couldn't lose my nerve now. The line connected, and after two rings, I heard the familiar groan of annoyance before she said, "What?"

"Ashten, it's Amara. How's it going?" A flash of heat spiked through my body, causing sweat to build on my neck. I couldn't believe what I was about to do.

"How's it going?" she asked, her Hispanic accent thick and sleepy. "It's six in the morning, Amara. What the hell do you want?"

I should have considered that before calling. I would have had better luck calling Tora or Wesley. "I need you and the rest of the team to come to Cedarbrook. It's time we put our theories to the test."

The phone line was silent for so long that I checked to see if the call dropped. It hadn't. "Hello?"

"I'm sorry. I'm trying to figure out if this is real or not." I could hear rustling, as if she was getting out of bed, and then a harsh sigh. "Are you being for real?"

"I am. This was always the end game for us, and I think it's time. Our final review is coming up. Doing this experiment now and getting the research will only secure our funding."

She mumbled something in Spanish. Knowing Ashten, it's nothing nice. She only spoke in Spanish when she was talking mad smack. "You know Wesley is on probation."

Shit. I'd forgotten about that. "I'll call Professor Lang and see if we can get a research pass. He knows that our deadline is approaching." To that, Ashten snorted. We both know Professor Lang can be a major dick most of the time. "Meanwhile, can you gather everyone at the lab and start packing? I really need to do this, Ashten." I didn't like the desperation in my tone. It was too revealing, too needy. It wasn't me.

As I feared, Ashten picked up on it. "You good, Amara?"

I shook off my feelings. "I'll be better once we prove our theory right."

Ashten agrees to round up the gang and call me once they get to the lab. Meanwhile, I would have the pleasure of chatting with Professor Lang.

I waited until seven to call him, considering the early morning hour. No need to start on a sour note, not when I'm going to try and weasel one of my team members out of probation. Honestly, it wasn't even Wesley's fault. He just happened to be at the wrong place at the wrong time. It always seemed to work that way with him.

While waiting, I contemplated what I would say to my dad when I returned home. He couldn't stop me from doing the research, but he wouldn't be happy. He especially wasn't going to be happy when he found out I was going to invite Laken along. While Dad played civil with him in passing Mom's notes over, in all reality, he very much disliked Laken. It could be teetering on the edge of hatred.

It wasn't wholly Laken's fault, but Dad never saw it that way. He saw it as my boyfriend abandoning me when, in all reality, it was a mutual understanding. I never planned on living in Cedarbrook for life, and Laken couldn't see life anywhere else. How was that ever going to work? Best to cut the illusion quicker rather than later. Still, that cut had hurt deep.

Dad would have to understand that I had to do this, and he couldn't stop me. That was going to be easier said than done.

Unable to wait any longer and respecting the after seven a.m. request, I finally dialed Professor Lang. While it rang, I took deep, calming breaths. Everything hinged on this phone call. Without Wesley, we couldn't do the project.

"Professor Lang, speaking."

My heart hitched. "Professor Lang, it's Amara Hayes."

"Ah, Amara. I didn't see you before you had to leave. I've been wanting to pass my condolences. It's a tragic loss." Professor Lang was among the few people outside Cedarbrook to speak with my mother. Considering their different views and opinions, it had been a rather interesting conversation. I'd found it rather amusing.

"Thank you." Breathy pause. "Actually, her loss has spurred me in a new direction with my research project. With my funding deadline approaching, I'd like my team to come to Cedarbrook to test the Spectrometer."

"I see," Professor Lang drawled. "You do realize that Wesley Cummings is on probation and is not permitted to leave campus with equipment."

Deep breathe. "I do. However, I can't complete this experiment without him. I'm calling to ask for a research pass for Wesley. His terms of guilt were slight, but his asset to this team is not."

Silence. Oh, the gawd-awful silence.

"In light of certain circumstances, I will grant Mr. Cummings a research pass. However," he said, sternly. I knew better than to be hopeful. "You have two weeks. That is all the time I am granting you for this project, Ms. Hayes. Is that understood?"

Two weeks! "But Professor—"

"Two weeks, Amara. There's no negotiating these terms."

I sat there, stunned. How were we going to pull this off in two weeks? It didn't seem possible. Research teams typically received a minimum of six weeks, with up to a maximum of one year. Though most of those teams probably didn't have to ask for a research pass for a student on probation. Although again, it wasn't his fault.

"I understand, sir. Thank you." Plans were already starting to form. We had to get started as soon as possible.

"Amara," Professor Lang said so gently, I'm pulled from my racing thoughts. Were there more stipulations? "Take care of yourself and your team."

The request was a gentle plea. He knew all about my project and the measures we would have to go through to prove it. "I will, sir."

After disconnecting with Professor Lang, I immediately called Ashten. "Hola."

"Are you all at the lab?" I fired off, the urgency to get things moving pushing me into a panic.

"We're all here," Ashten answered.

"Good. Wesley, Professor Lang is giving you a research pass."

"That's great, but do you know what would have been even better?" he asked, his thick-cut tone full of sarcasm.

"What?" I questioned.

"A notice that this was happening to begin with."

That was fair. I did kind of push them into this without much consideration. "I'm sorry. Honestly, this wasn't my plan either. Not until things changed."

"What changed?" Ashten asked.

"I'll explain it all later. Right now, I want to apologize for throwing this at y'all last minute, but I hope you'll understand once we are finished." If things go the way I hope they do, everyone will have answers.

We collaboratively create a comprehensive checklist outlining all the necessary equipment to bring. After detailing numerous items, I find myself at a loss for anything else to add. "Is that everything we need?" I pondered.

"I believe so," Wesley answered.

"Are you sure? I don't want to get out there and set up only to forget some small detail." We don't have the time for that. Two weeks. While it's probable that a lot can happen in two weeks, it's also equivalent for nothing to happen.

"Amara, girl, chill," Ashten prompts. "We've got this. You focus on getting yourself together, and we will see you mañana." A quick click followed, and I huffed a laugh. Ashten was nothing if not feisty.

Starting the car and turning back toward town, I take a deep breath. Things were about to get messy.

Chapter Three

My stomach tensed, a new wave of anxiousness consuming me. It was stupid to be this nervous. I'd seen Laken twice since being back in town. Why would this time be any different? It wouldn't. So why was I being such a girl about it?

The familiar smell of oats and hay consumed my senses as the bells on the door gave a friendly warning to the workers. Customer service was Mr. Jones's number one priority.

The young girl behind the counter looked up from the ranch magazine she was reading and smiled. "How can I help you?"

"Is Laken working today?" A cool draft made me shiver.

The girl pointed to the back. "He's unloading pallets."

"Okay, thank you."

Walking back toward the feed stacks, I got an odd sense of déjà vu. The many times I'd walked back here to see Laken when we dated all rushed back to me. Some days, bringing him a coffee or a cold cola was the only time I'd get to see him.

I turn the corner and freeze, my breath hitching, my stomach returning to its tense state. Laken was picking up a large sack of oats, his cocoa skin stretched tight over his muscles. He slung the bag over his shoulder like it weighed nothing, while his tight shirt revealed how lean this daily task has made him.

When my eyes met his light grey ones to find amusement, I wished for death. He just bluntly caught me staring and was enjoying every minute of it. "Amara," he said with surprise. "You okay?"

Kill me now. "Yeah," I said, shaking my head, closing my eyes, and pinching the bridge of my nose. "I've got a bad headache and got a little wave of nausea. I'm okay, though," I quickly added when he started toward me with worry.

He puts the feed on top of the stack. When he turns back to me, he crosses his arms and gives me a hard look. "What's wrong?"

"What makes you think something is wrong?" Can't a girl just show up to say hi? Well, probably not if they've been gone for four years and was hell bent on leaving again as fast as she could.

Laken doesn't flinch.

"Okay, fine. I got to thinking after you left yesterday, and you're right. I do deserve the truth. But so does everyone in this town, which is why I've asked my team to come join me." Now that I've said all that and gotten down to why I'm here, I really want to run. This is nerve-wracking.

"Why are they coming here?" he asked.

"To help, which is why I'm also here with you. For the last four years, I've been working on a prototype that will prove ghosts are not real." As I expected, he hung his head and started to turn away. "Laken, listen. I need your help, too."

He stopped mid-turn. "For what? You know, I see it differently."

"Which is exactly why I need you. There. At the research site. Not that I..."

Laken laughed, obviously finding humor in my embarrassment. "I'm always available."

What did that mean? "Laken, I'm serious. I'm a scientist and am not biased toward just one side. I want all the data from every angle so there are no questions with the results."

His smug smile falls. "What do you need me to do?"

"Exactly everything you and my mom were doing in the forest." Regret settled in my soul as I think about Mom. She should have been the one I did this with. Then again, it probably would have strained our relationship to the breaking point. It was threads before.

"Amara, what exactly are you planning?"

I bit my lip. "My team will arrive tomorrow with our equipment. I plan to set up camp near Oak Hollow. I've only got two weeks to prove my theory, and I plan on succeeding." Again, the deadline weighed on me. Would it be enough time?

Laken's eyes narrow, and the timid grey of his eyes turns dark. "And what? You thought you could stop in here, ask me to tag along, and then ridicule me for two weeks while I put my whole life on hold."

He's right. I hadn't even considered what he would have to give up to come with me. Sure, I'd figured he would want to, but that didn't mean he could. Not knowing what to say, I whisper, "I'm sorry," and turn to leave. If I thought I was embarrassed coming in here, I'm even more so leaving.

Maybe Dad was right. Perhaps, Laken's no good for me.

"Dammit. Amara, wait!" Laken hurried to catch me as I was walking out the door.

I don't stop, not until he grabs me by the arm. His gentle tone was pleading with me to listen. "I'm sorry. Your Mom's death and then you being here has stirred up a lot. I'm sorry."

My eyes roamed the sidewalk, the stray pieces of oats and grains filling the cracks in the concrete. "I understand. Trust me." Coming back home without her here was one of the hardest things I think I've ever had to do. We may not have agreed on a lot of things, but I loved her deeply.

"Let me talk to Tom. I'm sure I can get some time off." Tom loved Laken and had been a great boss to him, but two weeks was a long time for a business to lose someone.

I braved a look up at him. His soft gaze made me cave from my guard. I had a feeling that when I left again, it would be in shattered pieces. "Thank you. You know I wouldn't ask if I didn't value your time and opinion. You were the closest to Mom. You know the research and the lore."

He reached out and took my hand. "I'm here for you, always."

After promising to call me once he talked to Tom, we parted ways on better terms than any time since I've returned. I don't know what that means for us, but it was scary. Another frightening thing was the next step in my plan.

It was almost lunchtime when I pulled back into the driveway. Six hours ago, I wouldn't be back until shiny Christmas lights adorned the porch railings. Yet, here I was, back and trying to find the words to explain it all to Dad. Liam John Hayes was nothing if not stubborn. What can I say – like father, like daughter.

I didn't expect Dad home until around five. The time between now and then was going to be tedious. What would I do besides worrying about what to say to Dad and how to handle the outburst I know he will have? Let's just say, there weren't enough distractions in the house to keep me from that round of torture.

After fetching a glass of water, I sat on the couch with my laptop. Surely, I could find something to occupy my time.

Three hours later, I'm sitting with my laptop asleep in my lap and staring blankly as my mind frolicked with my thoughts... again. Angry, I put down the computer and started pacing the living room. The time crunch was weighing down on me. I needed my team here yesterday. What if they forget something? I needed to give them a little faith. And what about Laken? He hadn't called yet.

As I stand by the window, the soft rays of the late afternoon sun filter through the curtains, casting a warm, golden glow over the room. The air was still, almost like time had decided to pause momentarily. My eyes wandered over the familiar objects, each holding its own story. My gaze fell on the shelf by the wall, where a small frame stood. It was an old picture that seemed to have a life of its own, as if the moment it captured never truly ended.

I reached out slowly, my fingers brushing against the worn edges of the frame. It was a photo of Mom and me, taken on one of those rare days when the world felt light and everything was right. I could almost hear her laughter echoing in my ears and see her eyes sparkling with that warmth only a mother can give. The picture was from a time when everything was simpler, a time before arguments, before goodbyes.

She was holding me in her arms, a smile on her face that was so genuine. My younger self, wide-eyed and full of wonder, looked up at her like she was my whole world. Maybe, back then, I didn't fully understand just how much she meant to me. Holding that picture, the weight of that love, of those memories, felt like it was pressing into my chest.

I sat there for a moment, letting the memories wash over me. I could hear her voice and remember the way she would brush my hair out of my face when I was upset. These little gestures seemed so small then, but now they felt incredibly precious. I closed my eyes for a second, allowing the nostalgia to fill me. A tear slipped down my cheek, but I didn't wipe it away. It wasn't sadness but a bittersweet happiness, knowing how deeply I had been loved.

The sound of gravel crunching under tires reached my ears just as I placed the picture back on the shelf. I glanced out the window and saw his old blue truck, the wear of its years well shown in the rust, dents, and faded paint. The engine cut off, and for a moment, everything went quiet. I swallowed, my throat tightening, and I felt a wave of nerves rush through me.

This was it. The moment I'd been dreading all day. It was time to tell him.

I stood frozen, as my heartbeat quickened and my palms started to sweat. He hadn't been the same since Mom passed away. He was quieter, more distant. It was like the light inside of him had dimmed. I hated seeing him like that. And now, I was about to make it worse.

The door creaked open, and I heard his boots hitting the wooden steps as he made his way inside. My breath caught in my throat.

"Amara," his voice came from the hallway, rough and questioning.

I forced a smile, even though my stomach was in knots. "Hey, Dad."

I could hear him pause at the door to the kitchen, as if he knew something bad was coming. He leaned against the doorframe, his hands in his jean pockets, eyes searching my face for an answer as to why I came back.

"What's going on? You okay?" he asked, his voice carrying that concern he always had for me, even when everything around him seemed to fall apart.

I took a deep breath, trying to steady my racing heart. I glanced down, suddenly feeling like a little girl again, standing before him with the weight of the world on my shoulders. The silence stretched out between us like a tightrope, each of us unsure of how to cross it.

"Dad..." I started, my voice shaking just a little. "I need to tell you something."

His brow furrowed, his eyes narrowing slightly as he stepped closer. There was no turning back now. "What is it? You're scaring me, kid."

I looked up at him, meeting his gaze. The lines on his face were deeper than I remembered, the tiredness in his eyes more pronounced. He was holding on to so much, and I could feel it in the air between us. I reached for his hand; my trembling fingers brushed his weathered skin.

"It's about Mom," I said, my voice barely above a whisper. "She sacrificed everything, including her life, and never found the truth."

There was a quiet pause before I saw the shift in his face. The way his shoulders tensed and his jaw tightened. His eyes flickered with uncertainty. For a brief moment, I wished I could take the words back. But I knew, in my heart, it was the right thing to say.

"And what truth is that, Amara?" His voice cracked slightly.

I took a steady breath. "I have to know the truth of what's out there. Mom abandoned us so many times to chase a stupid myth."

The room felt smaller, the air heavier. His hand tightened around mine, but it wasn't the grip of anger or frustration. It was as if he was holding on to me to keep from falling apart.

"If you do that, you could potentially prove your mother died for nothing." He suddenly let go of me and turned to stare out the window. "How will you live with yourself knowing you did that to her?"

His fists clenched at his sides, his face red with anger, the kind that made him look years older and more worn. He paced in front of the window and ran his hand through his hair in frustration. "You don't understand," he spat, his voice tight. "You weren't the one who—" He cut himself off, the words stalling in his throat, like they were too heavy to speak.

I knew what he wanted to say. He was the one who had found her. After decades of worrying she'd never return after one of her trips, his fear became a reality. And it wasn't just a wife he had lost. It was the person he had built his whole life with. But through his grief, he was forgetting I had lost her too. I couldn't keep pretending like everything was fine when it wasn't.

"I do understand," I said, quiet, but firm. "I understand more than you think." His gaze flickered toward me, raw and unguarded, but I didn't flinch. I couldn't. I needed to be strong for both of us. "You can be angry with me, Dad. You can hate me for this, but I have to do this. I need to do this for me."

The silence between us stretched, thick and uncomfortable. I felt like I was walking on fragile ground, and one wrong word could shatter everything. "Dad, I don't want to hurt you. I only wanted to let you know where I was going. I didn't want to do this behind your back."

He took a deep breath, trying to steady himself, though frustration was still in his eyes. "Where are you going?"

I exhaled, knowing this part would be the hardest. "Me, my team, and Laken are camping at the edge of Oak Hollow for the next two weeks. The university is giving me a tight deadline to test my spectrometer. It's a push, but I believe in us, especially with Laken's help."

I watched his face change; the tension never fully left, but something else crept in. He ran his hands through his hair again, his shoulders slumping slightly. "Laken," he whispered. "I should have known." He turned then to face me. "Are you ready for that?" he asked, his voice softer now, but with an edge of concern underneath.

I knew he was no longer talking about Oak Hollow. It was Laken. "I'm ready," I replied, locking eyes with him. I was prepared for whatever heartache I found. "I don't have a choice anymore."

He stood there, his lips pressed together tightly as he looked at me. His eyes flickered to the photo frame on the shelf, the one of Mom and me. I could see his mind racing, his thoughts turning over. I knew he feared I would end up like her.

I stepped forward and placed my hand gently on his shoulder. "You can be upset, but please don't be angry with me."

The silence stretched again, thicker this time. I could almost hear the words he was forcing himself not to say. The argument he wanted to have to stop me from going. Finally, he nodded once, not with agreement, but with a reluctant understanding, and placed his hand over mine.

"Just be careful out there, okay?" he said, his voice barely above a whisper.

My throat tightened. "I will, Dad."

Although the tension wasn't entirely gone, the shift felt significant. It was a glimmer of understanding that broke through the silence. It was as if we had taken the first step on a long journey, realizing that progress doesn't always mean closure. Sometimes, just starting to navigate the complexities of our emotions can be enough to ignite a spark of hope.

Chapter Four

The air was thick with the scent of pine and damp earth as we made our way to the campsite. I could just make out the gnarled trees of Oak Hollow casting their long shadows. The rustle of leaves, distant bird calls, and the creaking of branches seemed almost too loud, and a shiver ran down my spine.

Ashten was visibly tense, her wide eyes scanning the trees as if she expected something to leap out at her any minute. She kept muttering under her breath, clearly unnerved by the eerie silence of the forest. She was mumbling something in Spanish before turning to me and saying, "This place feels wrong." Her voice trembled slightly as she set down her backpack. "I don't know if I can do this."

I turned slightly away from her, trying to hide my own unease. Ashten wasn't exactly the outdoorsy type. She was more of a city girl with a love for art and street food than anything resembling camping. "You'll be fine," I reassured her, though I wasn't entirely sure. The woods here had a reputation for being strange.

Wesley, ever the cautious one, was taking everything in with a slow, deliberate pace. He adjusted the straps on his backpack, pausing to observe the surrounding forest. "We need to make sure the campsite's set up before it gets dark," he said, his voice low but steady. His calm demeanor always helped, even if I knew he was probably just as apprehensive as the rest of us.

Tora, as usual, said nothing. She simply moved to a spot near the campfire ring, setting down her things with practiced precision. Her expression was unreadable, but something about her quiet demeanor made me think she was the one most at ease here.

I began unpacking my gear. Soon, Laken would join us, but for now, it was just the four of us. We worked in silence as we unloaded the vehicles and started setting things up. The quiet of the forest seemed to set the tone.

That is, until a crow cawed and made us all jump.

Ashten let out a small laugh, trying to shake off the tension. "You know, I thought camping would be fun. Like those campfire stories and marshmallows. Not this creepy vibe." She shivered.

I shot her a grin, trying to lighten the mood. "You'll get used to it. It's just the forest talking to you."

"You know, I could have collected data and begun analyzing it back at the lab." Where Ashten lacked in engineering, she more than made up for in math and data management.

I pouted out my lip. "But it wouldn't have been the same without you here."

Wesley adjusted his glasses as he looked at Ashten. The silver wire frames complemented his dark skin and even darker eyes. It was a good look for him. "Yes, the constant whining would surely have been missed."

To this, she flipped him off while I laughed in agreement. It's what I loved about my team. While we all had our hangups, we all joked with one another and still came together when we needed each other. They were my found family I'd never had growing up.

Soon, our small campsite was starting to come together. The four one-person tents were spread out evenly through the campsite, giving us a nice distance from one another. We all may be friends, but space and privacy are precious.

Wesley was already knee-deep in the technical setup, carefully pulling pieces of the MES from its protective cases. The device was intimidating, with coils and wires that looked like something straight out of a sci-fi film. The research we were conducting here—mapping anomalies in the forest's electromagnetic fields—was groundbreaking, but it wouldn't work unless every component was flawlessly assembled. Wesley's meticulous nature made him perfect for the job, but I still couldn't help the nerves that crawled under my skin. If even one thing went wrong, it could throw off the whole experiment.

I crouched next to Wesley and began inspecting each piece as he handed them to me. My fingers ran over the components, checking for wear or defects, anything that could make this project fail before we even started. Every screw, every connection had to be perfect.

"Are you sure this thing's going to work?" Ashten's voice cut through the silence, and I looked up to find her sitting on a rock near the fire ring. She was attempting to build a fire. From the looks of it, I would have to help her tackle that next.

Wesley didn't even look up. "It'll work," he said, his voice calm as ever. "But if it doesn't, we'll figure it out. It's what we do."

I nodded, but I wasn't entirely convinced. It wasn't the technology I worried about. It was everything else. What if there was something we were missing in our calculations? Something the forest itself was trying to hide from us? What if nothing happened at all?

I pushed the thought aside and focused on the MES. It wouldn't be the machine's official name, but it worked for now. It's what late nights and a lack of imagination led four scientists to come up with. We were calculating mass and energy, and spectrometer just sounded good. So, MES it was. Geniuses we are.

I finished checking the final pieces as Wesley started to assemble the meter's base. Just as we were getting into a rhythm, a distant crunching sound came from the trail leading into the campsite. I turned to see Laken emerging from the forest with a large pack slung over his shoulder.

To my surprise, he wasn't alone.

Trailing behind him, looking somewhat out of place with her bright, mismatched clothing and wide eyes, was Cori. Her vibrant strawberry blond long hair was pulled in a tight bun, and she too carried a pack. Why had Laken brought her?

I straightened up, wiping my hands on my pants as I looked between Laken and Cori, trying to mask my surprise. "Laken. I didn't expect you to bring Cori?"

He flashed me a grin, shrugging casually. "She's a local. And, well, when I told her I was coming out here, she asked to tag along. She's interested in the project and could offer a," he paused, his sarcasm hitting the right note, "unbiased observation."

I seriously doubted that. Cori would take Laken's side without question. She didn't know my team and had no ties to the research.

Laken continued with a mischievous glint in his eye. "I thought having someone who knows the area would be good. She's got some knowledge of Oak Hollow's history, which could be useful. Besides, the more hands, the better, right?"

Cori offered me a polite smile but seemed content to stand back and observe. We were once close in high school, but a lot of time and changes have come between us since then. Sure, she could help with the lore and history, but I couldn't help but feel a flicker of doubt. We had come out here to gather data, not to bring in unexpected variables.

Wesley looked up from his work, giving Laken a quick nod of acknowledgment. "Cori, right? I'm Wesley. We're setting up the meter now. You can help with the rest of the equipment once we get the MES online."

Cori nodded, her eyes flicking toward the machine. "Looks impressive," she said softly.

It was impressive and something we've spent three years creating. "Yeah, it is. If everything goes according to plan, we should have some solid data in a few weeks."

The air was cooling rapidly as the sun dipped lower behind the trees, casting the camp in a soft, golden glow that slowly gave way to shadows. Laken had already begun setting up his tent, hammering the stakes into the soft earth with his usual precise movements. He moved with the practiced ease of someone who'd spent more nights in the wilderness than most people would care to admit.

"Need a hand with that?" I called over to him, still sorting through some of the smaller gear we'd brought.

He glanced up and flashed me a quick grin. "I've got it, but I'll take a hand with Cori's. She's probably going to need all the help she can get."

I laughed and watched as Laken worked. He wasn't the type to make a show of being the group leader, but you could tell he liked being useful. It made me feel like he was already a part of the team. Laken would help wherever he could.

I turned my attention to Ashten, who was standing beside the fire ring with a slightly dazed expression. Smoke filled the air around her, but no flames came from the wood.

"You need help with that?" I asked, stepping toward her.

She looked up at me with a dramatic sigh, her eyes narrowing. "Girl, I swear... this place," she waved a hand around, "is a freakin' horror movie set. First, the tent nightmare, and now I've got to choke on smoke while calculating what's wrong with this firewood."

I grinned at her. "It's not that complicated. You know wood, fire, and air."

Ashten crossed her arms and raised an eyebrow, her lips curling into that signature sass. "Air? Yeah, I'm real familiar with air. But tents? Tents? Nah, girl, this isn't my thing. We had real beds on campus, you know? Pillows, blankets, the whole nine yards."

I bit back a laugh, knowing this was just Ashten's way of coping with her discomfort. "Hey, trust me, this is all going to work out. Now, let's get this fire going."

She narrowed her eyes in suspicion before she gave an exaggerated shrug. "Fine. But if I end up in a murderous tent situation later, I'm blaming you."

"Deal." I grinned as I crouched beside her, carefully showing her how to stack the wood to allow the oxygen to feed the flame.

While we worked, I glanced over at Tora, who had silently begun unpacking the cast iron grill they'd brought along. She was already setting up a small cooking station by the fire pit. Even amid a chaotic, unfamiliar environment, Tora always seemed to find calmness. She was the rock that calmed us, fed us, and pushed us through the hard times.

Ashten's whining slowly turned into laughter as the wood caught flame, and the fire soon crackled with life. Before we could celebrate, Tora spoke up, her voice soft but firm, cutting through the noise of our makeshift campsite.

"I'm starting dinner," she announced, looking up from the grill with a small smile. "Anyone want to help?"

I exchanged a glance with Ashten, who seemed to have forgotten her grudge against the fire. She raised her hand dramatically. "Yes, please. I might not be good with camp life, but I am when food is involved."

I chuckled. "Same. We're lucky to have you here, Tora. I'd be eating a cold ham sandwich if left to my own devices."

Tora's lips curled into a smile that was almost as quiet as she was. "It's no trouble. I know a grill like the back of my hand." She motioned around the cooking station. "Tonight's menu is something special. You're going to love it."

The grill hummed to life, and Tora started slicing vegetables with the grace of a professional chef. The smell of sizzling onions and peppers soon filled the air, and for the first time since we arrived, the quiet of the forest seemed to lift.

Ashten leaned against a nearby tree, still eyeing the food with obvious hunger. "Okay, maybe I can get on board with this whole camping thing if Tora keeps cooking for us."

I couldn't help but laugh as I put another log into the fire. "She'll keep cooking. You'll just have to get used to the rest of it. The tents. The bugs. The creepy woods."

Tora's voice rang out from the grill, cutting through the conversation. "Keep your stomach full and you'll be fine. At least, that's what my grandma always said. You can face anything on a full stomach."

"I don't know about that," Ashten argued, but pepped up with, "But I'll happily try."

We settled in around the fire, the warmth from the flames mingling with the sizzling sounds of dinner. It was easy to forget that we were on the edge of something far stranger than any of us had anticipated. For now, though, we were a team. And honestly? With Tora's cooking, I figured we might just survive this whole creepy forest thing after all.

Little did we know, we were all wrong.

Chapter Five

The last traces of the golden-orange sunset were slipping away behind the trees. The fire in the center of our campsite crackled and popped, casting flickering shadows across our faces. We had just finished Tora's amazing dinner—spicy grilled fajitas, sautéed peppers and onions, and a perfectly seared steak that still lingered in the air with its smoky scent. It was the kind of meal you didn't expect in the wilderness, but Tora made it all seem effortless.

Ashten leaned back against her backpack, her eyes reflecting the firelight. She looked both content and a little restless. The forest around us seemed to stretch out endlessly, the dark shapes of trees swaying in the evening breeze. The silence was back.

"So…" Ashten broke the quiet, her voice cutting through the stillness. "I know Oak Hollow is supposed to be this spooky place, but what's the deal with it? Like, what's the real story? There's gotta be some creepy lore or something."

I shifted, glancing around at the others. Tora was cleaning the grill, Wesley was hunched over a notebook, probably jotting down something to do tomorrow, and Laken was leaning forward, eyes fixed on the fire, his expression unreadable. Cori stood quietly behind him.

Laken spoke first, his tone as even as ever. "It's not just folklore. There's a reason people avoid this place. Oak Hollow has a long history of strange events. A lot of it's tied to the land and the woods themselves. They say it's cursed, though no one can agree on why."

Ashten's brow furrowed. "Cursed?" she asked skeptically, but her voice had a hint of curiosity. "Like, bad juju or something?"

"More than that," Laken said quietly, his voice low and steady. He wasn't looking at any of us now, but staring into the fire, as if the flames held all the answers. "People used to live here. Long before it became a sort of off-limits area."

"What happened to them?" Tora asked, taking us all off guard. She was standing behind Wesley now and wiping her hands on a towel with an enthralled expression.

Laken shrugged. "No one really knows. One day a family lived here, and then one day they didn't."

I gave Laken a pointed look. "Don't be so dramatic. You know that's not the story."

"Yeah, well, the one *on record*," he said, making air quotes around the word, "doesn't make sense either."

"The woman's house burning and her leaving doesn't make sense?" His total disregard of evidence makes me question whether I should have included him. Perhaps Dad was right. This could have been a huge mistake.

"A record that was made six years after the incident occurred. Tell me how that's factual." He doesn't give me a chance to answer. He's ready to take his argument and send it home. "It's not. The *fact* is, they made that record so they could claim the land as government to control it. And when did that happen?" He taps his chin for dramatic effect. "Oh, that's right, after the second disappearance."

"Disappearance!" Ashten injects.

I sigh and get down to some of the lore. "There are old stories about people disappearing, whole family lines vanishing without a trace. At first, they thought it was wild animals, maybe some kind of predator. But as the disappearances kept happening, people started to suspect something more. They say the forest itself started taking people."

Ashten's eyes widened, and she let out a nervous laugh. "So, what? The trees *eat* people? This sounds like a bad B-horror movie."

"It's more like the woods take what they want," Laken said, staring at the fire again, his voice colder than I expected. "Some people claim to have heard voices in the trees. Others say they saw shadows moving when there was no one around. It's said that if you stay too long in Oak Hollow, the woods change you. You start hearing things, seeing things, and then, you just disappear."

"Laken!" I snapped. "That's not all true. There have been survivors."

His eyes met mine, and he smirked. Dammit. "Who came out uttering nonsense and not remembering anything, including where they were. Those survivors who you once claimed were doing it to get a rise out of the community."

My cheeks warm as anger storms through my body. "We don't know that they weren't."

A silence fell over the group then. Even Ashten seemed to take a breath, her earlier sassiness dimming a little as she processed the story and the tension between me and Laken.

Doing what she does best, Ashten decided to break the tension and throw hands. "Great. So, we're stuck here with the spooky trees that want to eat us *or* we come out a mumbling mess."

I snorted, trying to lighten the mood. "Welcome to Oak Hollow, where the trees aren't the only things that might bite."

Laken finally turned his gaze away from the fire, his eyes narrowing slightly as if considering something deeper. "It's not just the stories. People who get too close to the woods start losing time. Hours can slip by without them even realizing. There are reports from people who say they went into the forest for a short walk and came out days later, not remembering anything."

Cori's expression darkened, her usually serene demeanor slipping for a moment. "I've heard those stories. The local elders talk about the Hollow like it's some kind of trap. They say it watches you. And when you're caught, it won't let go."

The fire crackled louder, its orange light casting long, shifting shadows around us. The way Laken and Cori told the story, even I was getting chills. It was all a ploy to sow doubt in the others' minds. I was sure of it.

Ashten shifted, rubbing the back of her neck. "Well, that's comforting." She forced a chuckle, but it lacked the usual confidence in her voice. "So, what, we just hang out here, enjoy Tora's awesome food, and pray we don't get sucked into some time-warping, tree-eating vortex?"

"You might want to keep your prayers handy," Laken said, his tone almost too serious to joke about. "Because around here, nothing's certain. We'll just have to make sure we're prepared for anything."

I glanced around at the group. There was a strange calm about them, but I could feel the unspoken unease building. Oak Hollow was more than just a place. It was a mystery that none of us fully understood.

If we thought the daytime silence was bad, the nighttime silence was mind-consuming. The only sounds were the occasional rustling of leaves and the distant call of an owl. The fire had burned low, its embers casting faint, pulsing glows against the surrounding trees.

I lay on my back, staring at the dark canopy above, frustration curling in my chest. The look in Laken's eyes, the angry tension of his jaw, not to mention his counterarguments, made me furious. He wanted this. He wanted us here. Yet, here we were, and he acted as if I were the enemy. The more I thought about it the more pissed off I got.

Frustrated, I shoved off my blanket and sat up. The cool night air licked at my skin. Careful not to wake the others, I stepped over the scattered gear and crossed the small clearing toward Laken's tent. He was set slightly apart from the rest of us, positioned near the trees.

I hesitated for half a second before pushing forward. The tent's fabric rustled as I crouched beside the entrance, fingers tightening against the zipper. "Laken," I whispered, keeping my voice low but firm. It's met with silence.

Sighing, I unzipped the flap just enough to peek inside. The dim glow of a lantern flickered, casting soft shadows along the tent walls. Laken was awake, sitting with his back against his backpack, legs stretched out, staring at something in his hands. A notebook. He hadn't even bothered to acknowledge me.

Anger flared hotter. "Really?" I hissed, slipping inside and zipping the flap behind me. "You ask me to come out here, and now you're acting like I don't exist?"

He didn't even look up. "You shouldn't be awake."

"Neither should you." I crossed my arms, my voice sharp but quiet enough not to wake the others. "You've been avoiding me all day."

Laken exhaled slowly, finally closing the notebook and setting it aside. "I'm not avoiding you."

I scoffed. "Could've fooled me. And how about the way you were acting tonight? It's like you're waiting on go to contradict everything I say."

Silence stretched between us, thick and unyielding. His eyes flickered toward mine, something unreadable swimming beneath the usual calm.

"Now that you're here… I'm terrified," he admitted after a moment. "I know you don't believe all the lore behind the forest's history. That's fine. But I do, and I've seen it take your mother. I can't watch the same thing happen to you."

"Nothing is going to happen," I insist. "I'm not like my mother, Laken. I'm not going to run into danger blind." I playfully slap at his leg. "Remember, I'm too skeptical."

He doesn't crack. "You don't understand. Something is different."

I frowned. "Different how?"

He hesitated, running a hand through his hair before looking past me. "I don't know yet," he admitted. "But something's off. I can feel it."

A chill ran down my spine, but I refused to let it shake me. "Then talk to me. Don't shut me out. That's how people truly get hurt." Emotionally and physically. We both should know this real well.

Laken studied me for a long moment before shifting so he was leaning forward, his forearms resting on his knees. "There's something I haven't told anyone."

I stiffened. "What?"

His voice was quieter now, almost lost beneath the distant whisper of the wind through the trees. "After your mom died, I found another survivor."

My breath hitched. "Where?"

He nodded, his jaw tightening. "In Jessieville." That was an hour north of here.

"Was he from here?"

"No. The only reason I found him was because your mother had me look into missing reports within a fifty-mile radius of Oak Hollow. She believed more cases were tied to the forest than the authorities reported." He looked down at the notebook he had been reading. "She didn't trust them at all."

That I knew, all too well.

Laken swallowed hard, then looked back up at me. "Amara, the man I found was a living shell. I've read your mom's notes on the two survivors she witnessed, but it's nothing compared to witnessing it with your own eyes."

Unease settled in my stomach as my palms began to sweat. "What do you mean?"

Laken's fingers curled into his palms. "He didn't remember his name. Didn't remember where he'd been. But he knew things about the Hollow that no one should know. And when I talked to him..." He trailed off, his expression darkening.

"What?" I pressed, my heartbeat quickening.

Laken lifted his gaze to mine, and for the first time, I saw something I rarely ever saw in him. Fear. "He told me the forest whispered to him. It told him it wanted blood."

A shiver coursed through my body, but I paused. I recognized the fear etched across Laken's face; it mirrored the same dread I had witnessed countless times in my mother's eyes as she recounted the chilling tales of the forest. Yet, despite the echo of her warnings, I couldn't allow myself to be swayed. "There's—"

"Don't," he interrupted sharply, his voice laced with urgency as he shook his head vehemently. "Don't try to rationalize this. Something truly terrible happened to him, Amara. I saw it with my own eyes." His voice dropped to an almost inaudible whisper. "For the first time in my life, I am genuinely terrified of this forest. And having you out here with me is driving me to the brink of madness."

A knot of dread tightened as the full impact of his words sank in. The trees loomed outside, their gnarled branches entwined like skeletal fingers, and the encroaching darkness seemed to press closer, as if eavesdropping on our conversation.

I grappled with the realization that I was not just afraid of the dark woods surrounding us; I was haunted by a deeper fear—the unsettling thought that Laken might be right, that something unspeakable roamed among the trees.

Chapter Six

The morning sun barely cut through the thick canopy above, leaving the forest in a muted, golden haze. The air was damp with the lingering chill of the night, but the sounds of nature had returned. Birds chirped, leaves rustled, with the occasional crack of a branch in the distance. It was peaceful, almost deceptively so.

Wesley and I worked in focused silence as we collected sensors and replaced them with others. Each one was designed to collect different forms of data that we would analyze daily. Wesley's meticulous nature was focused as we made our way through the undergrowth. He was sure and precise. I watched as he knelt, adjusting one of the small black devices at the base of a gnarled tree. The green light blinked steadily, indicating it was active.

I walked a few yards away, setting up another sensor near the remains of an old, moss-covered fence post. The deeper we went into Oak Hollow, the older things felt. It was as if time had been stretching and folding over itself for decades.

As I adjusted the last sensor, I glanced at Wesley. "You think our equipment will interfere with my mom's light sensor camera?"

Wesley looked up from his tablet, where he was monitoring the live readings. His brow furrowed slightly. "Doubt it. Laken's EMF meters and thermal imaging won't mess with it either. But your mom's camera..." He hesitated, thoughtful. "It's different. You said she modified it, right?"

I nodded, brushing dirt off my hands. "Yeah. The original design could pick up certain light spectrums, but she altered the sensor to detect anomalies the human eye can't register. She believed that some energy signatures leave traces we don't usually see." I paused. "If anything is actually happening here, her camera might pick it up."

Wesley exhaled, tapping a few settings on the tablet. "That's the part that makes me nervous."

I frowned. "Why?"

He turned the tablet so I could see the fluctuating readings. "Because something's already here. These sensors should be picking up consistent data, but they're fluctuating. The environment is shifting in ways it shouldn't be." He pointed to a line graph spiking erratically. "See this? It's almost like something's moving through the readings, distorting them as it goes."

A chill crept up my spine as I stepped back and scanned the trees around me. "You're saying something is affecting the sensors?" I asked carefully.

"I am," Wesley answered. His voice was quiet but firm. "But we don't know if it's a natural occurrence or a reading error. Your Mom's camera could help. If it picks up light distortions the way you say it does, we might be able to gather some more data to get an affirmative answer."

I swallowed hard, my fingers tightening around the strap of my bag as I swung it around and placed it on the ground. "Then we'd better get that camera set up."

I pulled the camera from its bag. It looked like something from a sci-fi movie. It was a standard motion camera, but with more tech added to it. The one thing my mother gave me besides her dark hair and golden-brown eyes was her brain.

"The connections on these are amazing." My admiration makes Wesley pause.

"Have you never seen this before?" he asked.

I slowly shook my head. "She made it after I left home. I asked Laken to bring it."

Understanding settled on Wesley's face as he took the camera from me. "It's rather unique." As he studied its tailored design, he slowly began to step back from where we came. "I think we should mount it between S14 and S16."

After securing it to the tree, I crouched beside Wesley as he double-checked our sensors one last time when a sharp rustling came from behind us. Instinctively, my hand shot out, gripping Wesley's sleeve. He stiffened beside me.

"Hello?" I called. This was followed by a slew of Spanish by a voice I knew anywhere. "Ashten?"

She burst through the trees a moment later, her usually confident stride now tense with unease. Her dark curls were slightly disheveled, her expression tight. The firelight from the night before had made her eyes gleam with amusement, but now they were sharp with fear.

"You two need to hurry the hell up," she snapped, arms crossing over her chest. Her Spanish accent thickened with her unease. "I do not like this place, and I definitely don't like you two being out here alone." Her eyes roamed the forest without pause.

Wesley didn't look up from the tablet. "We're almost done."

"Almost isn't fast enough, cariño." Ashten shook her head, shifting from foot to foot. "I swear, the trees are watching us."

I exhaled, dusting my hands off as I stood. "It's just your nerves messing with you." A sense of déjà vu hit me and I shivered. I used to repeat that mantra to my mom almost daily. "Laken's stories last night didn't help matters," I muttered.

Ashten shot me a glare. "No, you don't get it. I kept hearing something following me on the way here. Like footsteps, but every time I turned around, *Nada*." She clenched her fists. "I don't do creepy horror movie crap, okay? We're supposed to be smart people. And smart people *leave* when the forest starts acting all 'come play with us forever.'"

I exchanged a look with Wesley. His jaw was tight, but he finally gave a short nod, closing the tablet. "Alright, we're done. Let's head back."

"Finally," Ashten huffed, turning on her heel. "Because if one more damn leaf crunches behind me when no one is there, I am out."

We gathered the gear and started making our way back to camp. As we walked, I couldn't help but dwell on what Ashten had said about feeling watched. I would never admit it to anyone else, but I'd had the same chilling feeling earlier. I know it's from the hype of the project and all the energy coming from the others, but still. It's an uneasy feeling.

When we make it back to camp, I'm surprised to find only Tora. She sat on a log, running a blade along the edge of her knife in slow, deliberate strokes. The steady *shhhk* of metal against metal was the only sound besides the distant rustling of leaves.

I scanned the camp once, twice. My chest tightened. "Where's Laken?"

Tora didn't even look up. "Gone."

Obviously. "Gone where?"

"Some old homestead," she said, finally meeting my gaze. "Cori went with him. They left not long after you did."

The world tilted. *No, no, no.*

My breath hitched as my stomach twisted painfully. I turned away, pressing my hands to my temples, trying to think. Why would he go there? He knew better.

Wesley stepped up beside me, his voice measured. "What's wrong?"

I couldn't answer. Not yet.

Ashten let out a sharp, disbelieving laugh, but there was no humor in it. "Of course, he'd run off to some creepy abandoned house. It's like his whole thing." She rolled her eyes, but there was an edge to her voice. "Seriously, what's the big deal? They'll be back."

I turned to her so fast she flinched. "You don't get it," I snapped, my voice shaking.

Everyone paused and watched me now, expecting an explanation for my outburst. I wasn't ready to talk about the truth, but I guess I didn't give myself any other choice.

My throat tightened as I forced out the best half-truth I could muster. "That homestead is dangerous." Without a second thought, I turned towards the path into the trees, my heart racing in my ears. I didn't speak the truth, but I knew it, and it put a new fire of fear in me. I couldn't lose Laken the same way. "I have to find them."

Wesley's hand clamped onto my arm before I could take another step. "Not alone, you're not." His voice was firm. He wasn't asking.

I shook him off, my frustration spiking. "Wesley, I don't have time for this."

"And I'm not letting you run off, not thinking straight." His eyes locked onto mine, unwavering. "I'm coming with you."

Ashten let out a sharp laugh. "Yeah, no. Absolutely not. I'm not going back in there." She jabbed a finger toward the trees. "That place is bad news."

I'm beginning to contemplate her involvement in this project. "Ashten, I—"

"No." She crossed her arms, her stance as stubborn as ever. "Call me a coward, I don't care. But I'm staying here."

"Let me finish," I exhaled sharply, trying to shake off the nerves crawling under my skin. "I never asked you to go. You're good."

Wesley grabbed his pack and pulled out the thermal analyzer. The small device flickered to life in his hands, its screen casting a dim glow across his face.

"If they're out there," he said, adjusting the settings, "this might help us track them faster."

I turned and started into the forest, Wesley falling into step beside me.

Ashten called after us, her voice tight. "If you're not back in two hours, I'm dragging Tora to come find your asses."

I lifted a hand in acknowledgment, but didn't look back. The forest swallowed us whole, the canopy above stretching like skeletal fingers, blocking out most of the light. Our footsteps crunched against the damp earth, the air thick with the scent of pine and decay. Wesley walked beside me, his thermal analyzer humming softly in his hands.

For a while, we didn't speak. The heaviness of everything sat between us like a storm waiting to break.

Wesley finally broke the silence. "So, what's the deal with this homestead?" His voice was careful, cautious. "I mean, besides the obvious."

I tightened my grip on the straps of my backpack, my stomach twisting. I needed to choose my words carefully. I didn't want him to know the whole truth just yet. "It's the epicenter."

Wesley frowned. "Epicenter?"

I nodded. "Everything weird that happens out here—people disappearing, the time loss, the voices—all leads back there." I hesitated, my pulse kicking up. I leave out the fact that it's the center of all my pain. "It's like the forest itself revolves around that place."

Wesley got quiet as he processed what I said. Then he muttered, "And that's where Laken decided to go."

I let out a sharp, humorless laugh. "Yeah. Like an idiot." An idiot who didn't even consider my feelings about going there. Obviously. He should know I want to steer clear of that place. And for good reason.

Wesley exhaled hard. "Great. Love that for us."

If he only knew how much I loved that. The thing I didn't mention to him was that's where my mother died. So yeah, the appreciation I'm holding toward Laken was anything but loving.

The trees began to thin up ahead. The closer we got, the more unnatural the silence became. Even the wind had died, leaving only the sound of our breathing and the distant hum of the device in Wesley's hands.

Just before we reached the edge of the homestead's property, movement flickered in the gnarled trees. I stopped short, my pulse spiking. Wesley did too, his fingers twitching toward the thermal screen.

A moment later, Laken and Cori emerged from the shadows.

I let out a sharp breath, my relief tangled with frustration. "Are you kidding me?" My voice came out harsher than I intended, but I didn't care. "What the hell were you two thinking?"

Laken paused before answering, exchanging a glance with Cori that sent a jolt of anxiety through me. Something was off. They both appeared different. The color was drained from Cori's face, her usually vibrant features now stark with tension; her jaw was clenched tight. Laken, usually brimming with that cocky bravado, avoided my gaze, his expression now shadowed by something profound and unsettling.

Wesley stepped forward, the thermal analyzer in his hands beeping steadily. The rapid beeps had subsided, the device now emitting a rhythmic pulse that filled the thick silence. "What happened?" he asked.

Finally, Laken turned his gaze toward me. When his eyes met mine, a shiver snaked down my spine. His fear was deeper than it had been the night before.

He wet his lips before whispering, "We're not alone out here."

Chapter Seven

Laken crouched by the fire pit, methodically stacking the wood. His movements were steady, but there was something off about him. He'd been quiet and thoughtful ever since we returned to camp. Cori sat on a log nearby, her arms wrapped around herself as she stared into the flames. It was as if the fire held answers she couldn't quite grasp.

Wesley, Ashten, and I exchanged a look. Their reaction was one of fear, but from what? Ashten mouthed, *I don't like this*. I nodded, agreeing. Something was off.

"Dinner," Tora announced. The heart-warming smell of chili comforted me as she held out a bowl. I greedily took it and thanked her.

Laken took a bowl but still looked hollow as he thanked Tora.

After taking a few delicious bites, I put my spoon down and stared across the fire at Laken. I've had enough of this nonsense. "Are you going to spill what happened, or are you going to keep sitting there looking pathetic?"

He's quiet for a minute but finally resigns with an answer. "We went to look for something." His voice was quieter than usual. "Your mother's EMF meter. It was never recovered."

Silence fell over the group, thick and suffocating. My stomach clenched. I knew where this was going and why Laken had been so quiet. Mentioning it would make the others question what happened to my mother— something I still didn't want to talk about.

Ashten, sitting cross-legged with her arms draped over her knees, frowned. "What do you mean recovered?"

Laken's gaze flicked up to meet mine. He wasn't going to say it. He would leave that up to me. My stomach dropped, and suddenly I regretted eating the chili.

I sucked in a breath and forced myself to meet Ashten's confused stare. There was no getting out of it this time. "My mom died there."

The fire crackled, but no one spoke as they looked to one another. Ashten blinked; her face unreadable for a second before my words hit her. "Wait... what?" She sat up straighter, her usual sarcasm absent. "You're saying—"

"Yes." I swallowed, pushing past the lump in my throat. "She died at the homestead."

Ashten opened her mouth, then shut it. For the first time since I'd known her, she looked lost for words. Tora's fingers twitched as she absently stirred her chili, and even usually composed Wesley shifted uneasily.

Laken exhaled slowly, rubbing a hand over his face before speaking again. "That's why I went." His voice was still distant. "To see if it was there."

Cori's voice was barely audible as she spoke for the first time since we found them. "I've never... I can't believe..." Her chin trembled.

A chill ran down my spine watching her as Wesley stiffened beside me. "You found it?" he asked.

Laken dropped his head. "We didn't find the meter, but we discovered something else."

I leaned forward, gripping the chili bowl even tighter. The fire cast flickering shadows across Laken's face, highlighting the strain in his features. His usual composed demeanor was cracked, his fingers twitching slightly where they rested on his knee.

"Laken," I pressed, my voice firm but edged with something close to desperation. "Tell me what happened."

His gaze flickered up to mine, something unreadable in his eyes. Before he could speak, Cori did.

"The screaming," she whispered. Cori sat stiffly, her arms wrapped around herself as if she were trying to hold in a tremor. Her voice was barely above a breath. "It started as a whisper at first," she said, staring into the fire as her eyes began to water. "Like someone talking just beyond the trees. But then... then it turned into something else."

Laken's jaw tightened. His knuckles were white where he clenched his fists.

Cori continued. "It was a woman's voice, shrieking like she was in pain. It echoed through the woods, bouncing off the trees. It sounded like it was coming from everywhere at once." She swallowed hard, her gaze flicking toward me.

Ashten let out a sharp breath, muttering a stream of curses in Spanish as she shook her head, her fingers gripping her jacket like a lifeline. "Oh, hell no! Nope. This is some horror movie *bruja* nonsense." She shook a finger between Laken and Cori. "And what kind of idiotas hear screaming in the woods and don't run?"

"We did," Laken said darkly. "The faster we ran, the louder it got."

The fire crackled, and for a moment, the weight of their words pressed down on all of us.

I exhaled, forcing myself to stay grounded. To think logically. "That could've been anything," I said, knowing I would be hit with some hard looks. "A wild animal. A coyote or—"

"No." Cori's voice was sharp, cutting through my rationalization like a blade. "That was not an animal." She turned to me, her eyes dark and serious. I could see there was no convincing her otherwise, so I stopped.

A deep silence settled over the camp, broken only by the steady crackling of the fire. I realized there was no need to argue. We were a group divided. Laken and Cori believed deep in the lore. Wesley, Tora, and I believed in science. While poor Ashten believed it all and just wanted to go home.

Laken's voice was stern when he finally spoke again. "We need to go back tomorrow."

Ashten's head snapped toward him. "I'm sorry, what?"

Laken ignored her and turned to me and Wesley. "I only had one thermal reader with me, but I managed to attach it to a tree before we ran." His voice was steady. "If anything was there, we might have caught it."

Ashten let out a sharp laugh. It was one of those laughs that wasn't really a laugh at all. "Oh, hell no." She stood, jabbing a finger toward Laken like she was ready to throw hands. "You wanna go back to the place where the ghost of some banshee lady chased your dumb ass out? That's your brilliant plan?"

Laken's jaw tightened, but he didn't back down. "I'm saying we need answers. Whatever is out there is real, Ashten. It wasn't just in our heads."

She threw her hands in the air. "Fantastic. We'll just waltz back into the death woods, set up shop, and wait for something to eat us!"

"No one is getting eaten," I said, finding the idea completely overdramatized. From the looks on everyone else's face, I was the only one.

Ashten whirled on me, eyes blazing. "You cannot seriously be considering this."

I hesitated. As much as I disliked the idea of returning, Laken had a valid point. Unanswered questions had always loomed around my mother's death. If something had been out there, we couldn't ignore it. Even if my thoughts leaned toward the idea of a psychotic mountain man, while everyone else was thinking of creepy ghosts.

The forest had a way of messing with you, even the brightest and brilliant ones.

"This is insane," she muttered, raking a hand through her hair. "You're all *insane*."

Then, without another word, she spun on her heel and stormed toward her tent, shoving the flap open with way more force than necessary.

A beat of silence passed before Wesley let out a slow exhale. "Well," he said, adjusting his glasses. "That went well."

I sighed, rubbing my temples. "I'll go talk to her."

Laken remained silent, as did Cori. I had a feeling none of us were getting much sleep tonight.

The fire crackled behind me as I approached Ashten's tent. The night air was cool, but I barely felt it. All I could feel was uncertainty circulating through my veins about what we were going to do. First things first, settling homebase issues.

I hesitated at the tent flap before tapping it lightly. "Ashten?"

No response.

I sighed. "Look, I know you're pissed, but I just want to talk."

A long pause. Then, finally, the zipper rasped open a few inches. One of her dark eyes glared up at me through the gap. "Talking doesn't change the fact that you guys are insane."

I huffed a quiet laugh. "No argument there."

She groaned before yanking the zipper the rest of the way. "Fine. Come in."

I ducked inside, sitting cross-legged near her as she pulled her blanket over her lap. The inside of her tent smelled like vanilla and the faint, lingering scent of campfire smoke. She wouldn't look at me.

"What's eating at you?" I asked softly. "Besides all the creepy vibes."

She let out a slow breath, staring at her hands. "I don't know if I can do this, Amara."

I studied her, searching for the truth in her voice. "You don't have to," I said carefully. "If you want to go home, no one will hold it against you."

She exhaled sharply, shaking her head. "That's not what I meant."

I stayed quiet, waiting.

She shifted, pulling at the loose threads on her blanket. "My grandmother was superstitious, alright. She followed all these old traditions—honoring the dead, leaving offerings, believing that spirits stayed behind if they weren't at peace." Her lips pressed into a thin line. "I always thought it was stupid. Some old-school nonsense to make her feel like she still had control over something."

I didn't say anything, just let her keep going.

"But then she died," Ashten said quietly, her voice almost lost beneath the sound of the wind outside. "And suddenly, I wasn't so sure anymore."

I frowned, leaning forward. "What do you mean?"

She swallowed, her fingers tightening around the blanket. "I don't know. It was just this feeling. Like maybe she was right. Maybe there is more to life after death than I wanted to believe."

A beat of silence passed before she let out a small, humorless laugh. "So, I packed my bags, left southern Texas, and moved to Tennessee for college. I had no idea what the hell I was doing with my life." She glanced up at me then, her expression vulnerable. "Then I heard about your project. For some reason, it felt right. Like I was supposed to be a part of it."

I stared at her, absorbing every word. I wanted to tell her how we couldn't have gotten this far without her, or how much her friendship meant to me. I stayed quiet. I knew she needed to sort out her thoughts.

"But now?" She shook her head, letting out a shaky breath. "Now, we're actually here in action, and it's not just a cool research trip anymore. It's real and it's terrifying."

I exhaled, nodding slowly. "Yeah. It is." Again, I think of how the forest can change people. It changed my mother. It's shook Wesley. It absolutely terrified Ashten. Before leaving campus, not one of us feared the unknown because we didn't believe in it. That's no longer the case for some of us.

We sat silently for a bit, the wind howling softly through the trees outside. Finally, I asked, "Do you still want to stay?"

She hesitated, but then her jaw set with determination. "I don't know. I want to find out the truth. I'm just scared."

I gave her a small, understanding nod and took her hand in mine. I could relate to that sentiment more than she would ever realize. "I know. I can't promise you won't be scared, but if we stick together, we'll figure it out."

She met my gaze, and for the first time that night, some of the fear in her eyes faded. "Thank you, amiga."

Maybe none of us were truly cut out for this endeavor, not even Laken. Each of us was carrying our own doubts and fears. Yet, despite the uncertainty and the daunting path ahead, we found ourselves undeniably rooted in the situation. There was no option to turn back. Our choices had led us here, and we could no longer escape the reality we faced. With each step forward, we could sense the stakes rising, urging us to confront whatever lay ahead.

Chapter Eight

Three days.

Three long, uneventful, frustrating days.

Whatever eerie presence had driven Laken and Cori out of the homestead had gone silent. No voices. No shadows. No anomalies in our data. Just the constant, unyielding presence of the forest pressing in on us.

The stillness was starting to wear on all of us. The initial excitement, coupled with adrenaline, had faded, leaving behind short tempers and restless energy.

Ashten had been extra snippy, rolling her eyes at almost everything Wesley said. Laken was quieter than usual, spending most of his time reviewing thermal readings that never changed. Cori had taken to pacing the perimeter of camp, muttering about how the energy of the place felt off, whatever that meant. Even Tora—usually the glue that kept us together—was keeping her distance, as if she could feel the cracks forming between us.

By the time dinner rolled around, the tension was thick enough to choke on. We sat around the fire, the warm glow flickering across our tired faces. Tora had made potato soup, but no one seemed interested in eating. We were too busy stewing in our thoughts.

Cori was the one to finally break the silence. "You know what's weird?" She poked at the fire absently with a stick, watching the embers spark. "How skeptical you are, Amara, considering your mom's beliefs."

My stomach tightened. Where was she going with this? And why all of a sudden be like 'let's attack Amara'?

The fire popped. Laken glanced at me from across the circle. I could feel the weight of his stare. I exhaled slowly. "She's why I'm skeptical."

Cori's head tilted as curiosity flickered across her face. "How so?"

I leaned forward, resting my elbows on my knees. "Because belief without proof leads to false conclusions. My mom was brilliant and could have done anything. Instead, she got lost in her theories. She wanted to believe so badly that she stopped questioning." My throat tightened. "Look where that got her."

Silence fell over the group. No one needed me to say it. We all knew where it had led her. Her death.

Ashten cleared her throat. "Okay, but let's be hypothetical. You're saying ghosts don't exist at all? What about all the people who swear they've seen things? That they've felt something?"

I sighed, knowing this would turn into a debate whether I wanted it to or not. No matter what Ashten thought, I knew what Laken and Cori believed. "People experience something, sure. We sense things all the time, even in the safety of our home. That doesn't mean what they experience is real."

Cori scoffed. "Spoken like a true scientist."

"Thank you," I shot back.

Wesley, who had been mostly quiet, finally chimed in. "She's right. There's actual science behind why people think they see ghosts." He set his empty bowl aside. "One of the most common explanations is sleep paralysis or hypnagogic hallucinations. It's basically dreaming with your eyes open. It happens during REM sleep, when your brain is still in a dream state, but you're awake enough to see the real world layered over it."

Cori frowned. "So... your brain is just making stuff up?"

I nodded. "Essentially, yeah. And it's not just sleep. Exhaustion and stress can cause full-blown hallucinations, too. When people see faces in trees or shadows moving, they assume it's something supernatural. The truth is, our brains are wired to find patterns even when none exist."

This catches Laken's attention. "You're talking about pareidolia."

I nodded again, grateful for the backup. "Exactly. The human brain is built for recognition. It's why we see faces in clouds or hear voices in static. Our minds want to make sense of the chaos."

Ashten crossed her arms. "So, what? You're saying if someone feels like their dead grandmother is watching over them, it's all in their head?" I hate the hurt in her tone.

"Not exactly," I said carefully. "It feels real because the brain is filling in the gaps. The vast majority of perception isn't actually what we see; it's what our brain expects to see. It's called top-down processing. Our minds add details, emotions, and assumptions based on experience and belief."

"So, if someone sees a ghost," Cori mused, seemingly unconvinced, "it's really just their mind playing tricks on them?"

"That's the most logical explanation," I confirmed. It was not well received.

Ashten let out a frustrated laugh, shaking her head. "Damn. That's depressing."

Laken leaned forward, his eyes dark in the firelight. "That's a nice theory, Amara. Neat. Clean. Wrapped up in a perfect little scientific bow." He tilted his head, studying me. "But it doesn't explain everything."

I crossed my arms. "It explains more than believing in ghosts ever will."

His lips curled into a smirk, but something sharp was behind it. "Really? Then explain this." He sat up straighter, eyes locked onto mine. "If all of this is just misinterpretation, hallucinations, exhaustion—whatever you want to call it—then why do multiple people report the same experiences before ever hearing the stories? Why do sensors, thermal imaging, and electromagnetic meters pick up anomalies? Are you saying the equipment is hallucinating too?"

I clenched my jaw. "There are logical explanations for all of that. Environmental factors, interference, even data corruption—"

"Environmental factors?" Laken scoffed. "So, the scream Cori and I heard was what? The wind? A coyote?"

I fisted my hands, frustrated, but kept my voice steady. "It could've been. People hear what they expect to hear. Ever heard of auditory pareidolia? Your brain takes random sounds and assigns meaning to them. Static becomes voices. Wind becomes whispers. It's psychological."

Laken let out a dry laugh and shook his head. "That's convenient. So every single person who's heard voices in Oak Hollow just happened to be primed for it? Just a coincidence?"

I opened my mouth to argue, but he didn't let me.

"And what about time loss?" His voice hardened, his smirk fading. "That's not just 'seeing faces in trees.' People have walked into these woods and *lost* hours. People who don't believe in ghosts. People who had no reason to expect anything strange."

My pulse kicked up, but I kept my expression neutral. "There are medical explanations for that, too. Dissociation, amnesia, even infrasound can cause a feeling of distortion."

"You have an excuse for everything, huh?" He exhaled sharply and shook his head. "You keep talking about logic, about science, but what happens when logic isn't enough? When the evidence doesn't add up, and you're standing in the middle of something you can't explain?"

The fire crackled between us, flickering shadows across Laken's face. I could feel everyone watching. Their gazes shifted between us like we were about to snap.

Ashten muttered something under her breath and shook her head. "This is getting way too intense, guys."

But Laken wasn't backing down, and neither was I.

I took a slow breath, gripping my knees. "If you want to believe in ghosts, Laken, go ahead. Just don't expect me to."

His eyes darkened, and for the first time, his voice dropped low. "I don't want to believe in anything, Amara. But I can't deny it either."

A profound silence enveloped us, thick enough to feel almost suffocating. Each breath seemed to echo in the stillness, and no one dared to speak. The night sky loomed above, its inky blackness punctuated by distant stars.

Deep inside me, a flicker of turmoil stirred. Despite my attempts to shove it aside like a forgotten memory, I couldn't shake off the unsettling truth buried within Laken's words. They clung to me, persistent and inescapable.

I had long wanted to reject everything, preferring the comfort of disbelief. Yet, in Oak Hollow, an inexplicable force tugged at my resolve, turning the very act of denial into an uphill battle. It felt as if the town itself was alive, whispering secrets that beckoned me to listen, to see. Something within its shadows made it increasingly difficult to ignore the stirring belief that perhaps, just perhaps, there was more to this world than I had dared to imagine.

Chapter Nine

The winding road twisted and turned as we climbed the hill. When we finally reached the crest, the charming town of Cedarbrook spread out before us in a breathtaking view. Located in the cradle of the valley, the rooftops glimmered in the soft morning light, their warm hues of terracotta and cream contrasting beautifully with the deep greens of the surrounding landscape. The streets, lined with quaint houses and small shops, meandered gracefully through clusters of trees. The branches were heavy with budding blossoms that hinted at the arrival of spring.

As I took in the vibrant scene before me, the nagging weight pressing down on me began to dissipate. I momentarily cast aside the tension and frustration that had overshadowed my thoughts in the days prior. The beauty of Cedarbrook wrapped around me like a comforting embrace, offering a brief respite from everything I had been carrying.

"I forgot how beautiful it was," I admitted, my voice softer than I intended.

Laken, who had been quiet most of the drive, glanced at me. "Yeah." His fingers flexed against the steering wheel. "It's easy to forget until you see it again." From his tone, I didn't know if he was talking about the town or something else entirely.

I adjusted in my seat, eyes locked on the view ahead. I'd wanted to come alone, to have a break from everything, especially him. But of course, Laken had insisted on tagging along. Maybe he thought I'd get lost or not come back. There had been no rhyme or reason other than his demand that he was coming with me.

The silence stretched between us as we drove down the hill, the tires humming against the pavement. The closer we got to town, the heavier the air inside the car felt. I knew I should say something, but I didn't know what. We haven't spoken since the disagreement the night before. Picking up where we left off wasn't the conversational piece I was looking for.

"I've missed you," Laken whispered.

All thoughts of speaking halted. I blinked, turning toward him. His gaze was still on the road, his expression unreadable, but his grip on the wheel was tight.

I swallowed hard. "Laken—"

"I know things are different now," he continued, his voice steady but laced with something else. "I get why you left. Why you don't want to be here. But I mean it. I've missed you."

Something twisted in my chest. He said it so simply, like it wasn't something that could shatter between us.

I turned my gaze to the window, where the familiar streets and storefronts blurred past us. "You make it sound like I just vanished into thin air," I murmured, my voice barely above a whisper.

"Didn't you?" he replied, a note of pain lacing his words. The hurt in his tone was unmistakable.

I exhaled sharply, gripping my knee. "It wasn't that simple."

"Maybe not for you." His words were quiet but sharp, cutting through the space between us. I felt the weight of them, of the things we weren't saying, and for a split second, I considered telling him the truth. About why I really left. About why being back here felt like standing at the edge of something too deep to climb out of.

I didn't.

Instead, I kept my eyes on the road ahead, watching as Cedarbrook pulled us back in.

The small talk we made in the grocery store was that of strangers. We loaded the last of the groceries into the truck in silence, the plastic bags rustling as Laken shut the tailgate. The sun hung high, casting sharp shadows across the pavement. The trip into town had been uneventful, aside from the unspoken words between us.

But we weren't done yet. I sighed, already bracing myself for what was next. "Let's stop at Dad's before we head back."

Laken gave me a sideways glance but didn't argue.

Dad's house was the same as always. It was worn, familiar, and perpetually caught between tidy and cluttered. Tools were scattered across the back porch worktable, and the faint scent of coffee drifted from inside.

When we stepped through the door, Dad barely looked up from the newspaper spread across the kitchen table. His grumble of acknowledgment was the closest thing to a greeting we'd get.

"Didn't expect you back so soon," he muttered, flipping the page. "Thought you'd be too busy running around in those damn woods."

I sighed, dropping the bag of coffee and canned goods on the counter. "Nice to see you too, Dad."

Laken, to his credit, stayed quiet.

Dad finally looked up, his eyes narrowed. "Still think this project of yours is a good idea?"

"Yes," I said, keeping my voice even. "And it's going fine."

"Hmm." He didn't look convinced. "Well, don't come crying to me when it turns sideways."

I rolled my eyes and walked over, pressing a quick kiss to his cheek. "Everything's going to be okay."

Dad scoffed, but there was something softer in his expression. It said he wanted to believe me, even if he couldn't.

"Look, Dad, I wanted to say—"

He suddenly snapped his fingers. "Oh, I almost forgot." He stood from the table, completely shouldering the apology I was trying to give him. When it came to a breath of genuine emotion, he skirted around it as best he could. "I found something the other day." He reached for a worn envelope on the counter and held it out to me. "Thought it might've fallen out of one of those boxes I gave Laken."

I frowned and took it. The paper was aged and fragile. As soon as I saw the handwriting, my stomach clenched. It was my mother's.

My hand began to shake as I unfolded the note. My eyes scanned the words scribbled in hurried, slanted script:

Those who trespass will lose their way and wander until the forest claims them. And if their blood bleeds true, may they find their damnation.

My breath caught, and I reread it. Once. Twice. The words were digging into my skin like thorns.

"What is it?" Laken asked, stepping closer and peering over my shoulder. A chill consumed me as his breath fanned over my skin.

My heart pounded as I stood there trying to make sense of it. Mom had written this, but why? And why the hell did it sound like a warning?

I folded the note carefully and tucked it into my jacket pocket as I turned back to Dad. He was already settling back into his chair, his expression unreadable.

"Thanks for this," I said, although my mind was elsewhere. I didn't want to alarm him more than he already was. "Dad, like I was trying to say earlier—"

He waved his hand, cutting me off again. "Let's not do this now, kid. Just focus on coming home safe."

I wanted to disagree and tell him what was going on. What if I didn't make it back? Stranger things happened. But then I realized that Dad couldn't admit to that fear, especially after losing his wife so suddenly. He needed me to fight to make it home, no matter the cost.

I reached out and placed my hand on his arm. "Okay, Dad."

He just grunted in response. "Be careful, kid."

I smiled. "I will."

Laken and I stepped out onto the porch, the late afternoon sun stretching long shadows across the yard. Neither of us spoke as we climbed into the truck, the doors slamming shut in unison.

As Laken started the engine, I finally broke the silence. "Is Mom's journal still back at camp?"

He shot me a glance, clearly not expecting the question. "Yeah. Why?"

I pulled the note from my pocket, staring at the words again. I wish I could make them make sense. "This has to mean something," I murmured. "Mom wasn't the type to just write cryptic messages for no reason. There's a connection here. I'm just not seeing it."

Laken drummed his fingers on the steering wheel, skeptical. "Even if it means something, how do we figure it out?"

I looked over at him. "Wesley."

His brow furrowed. "Wesley?"

I exhaled slowly, my mind racing. "Look, Wesley is a freaking genius—like, insanely good. I want him to read both this note and Mom's journals. Maybe he can decipher something we're missing."

Laken's eyebrow arched. "Wesley? You really think his technical brain can crack something so lore-heavy?"

I gave a small, determined shrug. "He doesn't have the personal baggage or the old superstitions to get in the way. He sees the world as data, patterns, and facts. That could be exactly what we need."

Laken fixed his eyes intently on the asphalt stretching out before us. The tension in his voice was palpable as he said, "I don't know." A note of hesitation lingered. His reluctance wasn't an outright dismissal, though.

"It's worth a shot," I pressed, hoping to inject a sense of optimism.

He looked back at me and nodded slowly, a sign of his trust in my judgment. "If you trust him, then I trust him too. We'll let Wesley take a crack at it." There was a hint of resolve in his voice, and I couldn't help but feel a surge of relief wash over me.

I smiled fondly at him, grateful for his support. His words echoed in my mind. *I missed you.* It was a gentle reminder of what we had lost and what we were rediscovering.

Gathering my thoughts, I took a deep breath and tried to push my emotions aside. I needed to concentrate on the road ahead. We had a plan to follow. We would head back to camp, present all the notes and journals to Wesley, then devise a solid plan of attack based on what we learned.

Yet, beneath the surface of my determination, I felt an unsettling awareness. There was a relentless ticking of a clock that echoed in my mind, reminding me that time was slipping away. The weight of urgency settled heavily on my shoulders, propelling me forward with each mile we covered.

Chapter Ten

The truck barely rolled to a stop before Ashten came sprinting toward us, her face pale, eyes wild with panic.

"She's gone!" she gasped, gripping the door before I had time to step out.

A wave of dread slammed into me, sending my stomach plummeting into a whirling void. "Who's gone?"

"Cori!" Ashten answered, distressed. "We thought she was just sleeping in, but when lunch came around, we went to check on her. She wasn't there. We searched the whole camp, and then Tora and Wesley went looking for her. They haven't come back either!"

Laken released a soft curse, frustration lacing his words as he sprang into action. His boots thudded against the gravel as he moved with urgency. I barely registered his movements as he quickly rifled through the cluttered back of the truck, pulling out his gear.

I turned my attention back to Ashten, whose gaze was fixed intently on the horizon. Fear was etched across her features.

"How long have they been gone?" I questioned.

Ashten shook her head frantically. "I don't know, maybe two hours? I waited here, hoping they'd come back, but they haven't." Her eyes filled with tears. "I didn't know what else to do."

I gripped her shoulders and forced her to look at me. "Okay, breathe. We're going to find them. I promise."

Laken slammed the tailgate shut, his jaw set. "We need to move now. The sun will set in a few hours."

I nodded slowly, a flicker of resolve in my gaze. An unsettling shiver of fear crept along my spine like icy fingers. My heart pounded, every beat echoing the urgency to move faster. I took a deep breath, inhaling the scent of damp earth and pine and forcefully pushed the panic back down. There was no time for hesitation. Cori was out there, somewhere in the vast expanse of shadow and uncertainty, and so were Tora and Wesley.

"Get whatever you need," I told Ashten. "We're not coming back until we find them."

She swallowed hard but nodded, running to her tent. Laken met my gaze across the truck, his expression dark. "Are you sure she should go?"

I'm sure he's thinking of her fear the other night as we discussed going back into the forest. I couldn't blame his hesitation. I had my own. "I'm not leaving her alone considering her current state and you're not going alone. Therefore, the only option is for her to go with us."

Laken's jaw was tight as he adjusted the straps on his pack. His voice was firm, but I caught the flicker of unease in his eyes. "Cori went to the homestead," he said. "She must've gone after the camera."

I clenched my fists tightly, feeling the rough texture of my palms as my frustration bubbled to the surface. "Alone? Why would she do that?" I asked, my voice sharper than I intended. My mind raced, thoughts spiraling in a chaotic whirlwind as I tried to piece together the fragmented puzzle of our situation.

"And if she did go to the homestead, where the hell are Tora and Wesley?"

Silence followed my panic as the three of us exchanged worried glances. No one had an answer to my desperate questions.

The deeper we ventured into the forest, the more unnatural everything felt. The air itself was thick, heavy with something I couldn't name. The towering trees swallowed the last of the sunlight, leaving behind only dusk's dim, shifting glow. Every step we took felt like we were sinking deeper into something alive, something watching.

Fear was clouding my thoughts, making it difficult to think clearly. I struggled to grasp something solid, a fact that could center me. The silence was too loud, too piercing.

A sudden scream shattered through the air. It was high-pitched, human, and filled with desperation. The sound came from our left.

Ashten gasped, spinning toward the sound. "Oh my god—"

Another scream echoed from the right. Then, another followed.

They overlapped, distorted, and twisted, echoing through the trees like a chorus of agony. The hair on the back of my neck stood up. It wasn't just one person screaming; it was multiple voices. No, wait. It was the same scream, thrown in different directions, played on a loop like a nightmare stuck on repeat.

A deep, rhythmic knocking suddenly broke through the chaos.

Crack.

The sharp, resonant sound of wood slamming against wood echoed around us, clear and purposeful. It originated from a point ahead, reverberated from behind us, and then abruptly shot to our right. Each thud seemed to carry a weight of intent, filling the air with anticipation as we tried to pinpoint the source of the unsettling noise.

Crack. Crack.

Logic. There was logic to this. Yet, despite knowing this, my mind couldn't focus on the truth.

A whisper slithered through the trees, too low to understand, too close to be imagined. I turned sharply, scanning the dark spaces between the trunks, but saw nothing.

Ashten made a strangled noise in her throat, her breath coming in sharp gasps. "No. Nope. Nope!" Her hands shook as she clutched the straps of her backpack. "I can't. I'm not doing this." She turned and ran.

"Ashten!" I lunged for her but missed as she tore through the underbrush, branches snapping in her wake.

More screams answered her. Louder now. Closer.

I spun back to Laken. "We have to go after her!"

He grabbed my arm, his grip like iron. "No! If we chase her blindly, we'll get separated too!" His voice was sharp, but I could see the fight in his eyes and the way his chest rose and fell too quickly. He was just as scared as I was.

Tears stung at the backs of my eyes. "I can't just let her go!"

A spine-chilling scream echoed through the dense forest, slicing through the air like a dagger. This time, it was not Ashten's voice that rang out. It belonged to something far more unsettling. The sound was deep and guttural, a haunting imitation of a human cry that seemed to falter and twist as if the creature attempting to produce it could not fully grasp the nuances of human expression.

Laken's fingers twitched against my arm.

"Ashten!" I screamed into the trees. My voice felt swallowed up by the overwhelming noise, the unnatural chorus of screams, knocks, and whispers.

No answer.

Just more *crack. Crack. Crack.*

Then, the forest fell silent.

No wind. No leaves rustling.

Just stillness.

I swallowed hard, my breath shaking. "Laken?"

His grip on my arm tightened. "We need to move. Now."

I turned back toward the direction Ashten had disappeared into, every instinct screaming at me to chase after her. But I couldn't see anything past the thick, endless maze of trees. If we ran mindlessly, we might never find our way back.

My stomach twisted into knots, a painful reminder of the tension that gripped me. Ashten was a fighter. I had to cling to the hope that she would navigate her way back to camp safely.

Then, from the depths of the trees, a new sound broke the stillness. It was soft yet rhythmic, footsteps drawing nearer with an unsettling steadiness. Whatever was approaching us moved deliberately, each step echoing in my chest as my heart raced.

"Laken," I whispered, my voice barely escaping between clenched teeth as the branches rustled ominously nearby.

Suddenly, Wesley stepped into view, emerging from the shadows of the forest. His face was ghostly pale, his movements sluggish and unsteady. For a heartbeat, the air around me thickened, and I couldn't catch my breath. The slow, purposeful footsteps had conjured the worst possible scenarios in my mind. I had to regain my composure, to push away the dread clinging to me like a second skin.

Laken and I stood frozen as Wesley came into view. His arms were outstretched slightly to feel his way forward. The last of the sun's rays was barely a flicker in the sky. I pulled out my flashlight to find why he'd been walking so slowly. He had no flashlight.

Relief surged through me. "Wesley," I gasped, stepping toward him and embracing him. "Where's Tora?"

He just shook his head, breathless. "We got separated."

The relief ebbed. "What?"

Wesley braced himself against a tree, wincing as he shifted his weight. Blood soaked through the denim of his jeans, glistening in the dim light.

"You're hurt," I said, my voice barely above a whisper.

He nodded, swallowing hard. "Fell down a ravine. That's how I lost my flashlight. We were looking for Cori and following this weird sound when the screams—" His voice caught. He closed his eyes for a second before shaking his head. "It messed with us. Disoriented both of us."

I stepped closer, hands trembling. "How bad is it?"

He exhaled sharply, then lifted the fabric of his jeans just enough for me to see the deep gash along his leg. The blood had slowed, but it wasn't stopping.

"Jesus, Wesley," Laken muttered. "You need stitches."

"No shit," Wesley gritted out. "But it can wait. We have to find Tora and Cori."

I clenched my jaw, my mind spinning.

Laken ran a hand through his hair. "We need to get him back to camp first. If he loses too much blood—"

"No." Wesley shook his head, eyes fierce. "Tora is still out there. I'm not leaving her."

They both looked to me for a decision. I was going to have to make a choice, one I didn't know how to make. Stay and look for the others or get Wesley back to camp before he bled out.

Before I could gather my thoughts and decide, a different sound sliced through the stillness of the night. Laughter. It was bright and infectious, ringing out into the darkness. It was unexpected, a stark contrast to the quiet that had enveloped us moments before, and it made the hair on the back of my neck stand up. I shivered.

Laken's expression hardened, his jaw clenched as he turned toward the sound. His fists were tight at his side. What was he going to do, fight the thing? That eerie laughter still floated through the trees, unnatural and distant, yet too close all at once.

I swallowed hard and turned to him, my voice barely steady. "What are we going to do?"

For a second, he didn't answer. His eyes scanned the trees, his body tense like a predator sensing a trap. Then, his gaze flicked back to me. "We get Wesley back to camp, patch him up, and then we go after Tora. We can't afford to split up again."

Wesley stiffened. "No. I can still—"

"Wesley, you're bleeding out," Laken cut him off, his voice sharp but controlled. "You can barely stand. You're no good to Tora like this."

Wesley opened his mouth to argue, but a new sound rippled through the trees. It was a soft rustling, almost like footsteps weaving through the undergrowth. They weren't steady. They were erratic. Stumbling.

I sucked in a sharp breath. "Tora?"

Laken motioned for me to stay put, then carefully stepped forward, listening. The laughter had stopped, replaced by an eerie silence that was almost worse.

Then, through the gaps in the trees, something moved.

A shadowy figure staggered between the trunks, unsteady and slow. My breath caught as the shape lurched into a sliver of light. It was Tora, but not the Tora who had handed me a sandwich and wished me luck earlier in the day.

Her head was bowed, her arms hanging limp at her sides. Her hair was wild, tangled with leaves, and her clothes were torn. She moved like a puppet with cut strings, her steps dragging like she wasn't fully in control of her body.

"Tora!" I called out, my voice echoing in the stillness, shattering the paralyzing grip of fear that had seized me moments before.

Her head whipped around in an instant. A chill crept down my spine as I gazed into her eyes. They were unsettling—too wide and too dark, like the depths of an abyss that had consumed all light. It felt as if night itself had crept in and taken residence behind those once-familiar blue irises.

Then she smiled at me. It was not the joyful, welcoming smile I had hoped to see. No, this grin was unnaturally wide, stretching far beyond the bounds of comfort. It was a distorted expression, a mask that hinted at something sinister lurking beneath the surface.

Something was profoundly, irrevocably wrong.

Chapter Eleven

The wind died all at once.

Tora's body, suspended like a marionette, suddenly dropped. She crumpled to the ground like a lifeless doll. My heart slammed against my ribs as I ran to her, sliding onto my knees beside her still form.

"Tora?" I called her name, my voice thick with anxiety. My fingers trembled as they pressed against her neck, searching for any sign of life. I felt a pulse. It was faint, but steady. Her chest rose and fell in shallow breaths. A wave of relief washed over me, but it was overshadowed by the weight of uncertainty we faced.

"We need to get back to camp," Laken said, his voice urgent but controlled. "Now."

"What about Cori and Ashten?"

His jaw tightened, his eyes flicking warily toward the trees. "We'll come back for them. We can't take care of them if we're dead on our feet. Tora and Wesley need help now."

I wanted to argue, but a sharp stab of fear lodged itself in my throat. Laken was right. Wesley was barely standing, and Tora... we didn't know what had just happened to her, but she needed to be stabilized.

Laken didn't wait for my response. He crouched, scooping Tora effortlessly into his arms, adjusting her so her head rested against his chest. In the dim glow of my flashlight, I could see his arms tense with the effort of carrying her weight.

Wesley swayed, and I turned just in time to grab his arm before he lost his balance.

"Easy," I murmured, shifting so he could lean into me. His weight was heavier than I expected, his body sluggish with exhaustion and pain.

"Sorry," he mumbled, grimacing as he put pressure on his injured leg. "I think adrenaline was keeping me upright. Not so much now."

I tightened my grip on him. "Just keep moving. We're almost there."

Laken set a hard pace, navigating the uneven forest floor as quickly as possible without jostling Tora too much. I swore I heard whispers slithering between the trees every now and then, but whenever I turned my head, there was nothing. Just shadows. Just my imagination.

The warm, inviting glow of our campfire finally broke through the dense curtain of trees ahead. I felt an overwhelming urge to crumble to the ground in sheer relief, but I forced myself to remain steady. The familiar crackle of flames and the scent of burning wood should have washed away my anxiety, yet a persistent unease clung to me like a cloak.

Cori and Ashten remained out there, wandering in the vast darkness. Strains of unease coiled around me, tightening like a noose. Whatever presence had stalked us earlier, blending seamlessly with the rustling leaves and whispers of the wind, was still out there. My heart thudded relentlessly as I scanned the shadows, half-convinced that unseen eyes were fixed on me, watching from the depths of the night.

The morning light filtered through the trees, casting eerie shadows over our camp. Wesley sat near the fire, his leg stretched out in front of him. The blood-soaked bandages were stark against his pale skin. He looked exhausted but stable.

Laken knelt beside him, double-checking the wrapping around his thigh. "You're lucky," he muttered. "A few inches to the left, and we'd be dealing with something a hell of a lot worse."

Wesley huffed out a breath. "Feels bad enough already."

I glanced over at Tora, still lying unconscious on a sleeping pad we'd laid out for her. Her chest rose and fell steadily, but she hadn't stirred once since she hit the ground last night. Anxiety clawed at my stomach as I thought about the lifeless way she fell. How was she still breathing?

"We need to get her to a hospital," Laken said, standing up and wiping his hands on his jeans. "She hasn't woken up, and we don't know how bad her head injury is."

Panic flared inside me. "No," I said quickly. I'd feared Laken would push for this. The problem was, he didn't understand what it would do. "Not yet."

Laken turned to me, his face hardening. He looked at me like he didn't even know me. "Amara, we don't have time for this. People are missing. Tora could be seriously hurt, or did you forget the twisted way she hung in the air hours ago?"

I clenched my hands into fists, trying to keep my voice steady. "I haven't. But if we call for help now, the university will shut everything down. The project will be over. We won't get another shot at this." I felt like we were so close to discovering something, what I didn't know. I may regret finding out, but it was why we were here. It was all the hard work we'd put into our theories and machines. I wasn't prepared to easily flake on it all now.

Laken's eyes burned into mine, frustration and worry battling in their depths. "Amara, this isn't just about your project anymore," he said, voice low but firm. "Tora is unconscious. Wesley could've bled out if we hadn't found him. And Ashten and Cori—" He shook his head. "We don't know what's happened to them."

"I *know*," I snapped, wrapping my arms around myself in an instinctive attempt to ward off the fear trying to claim me. My fingers trembled uncontrollably, the anxiety coursing through me making it hard to concentrate. I clenched my fists tightly, desperate to quell the shaking. "But if we call for help, it's over. The university will shut us down, and I won't get another shot at this. Everything we've poured our hearts into, my mom's work, will be buried."

Laken ran a hand through his tousled hair, exhaling sharply in frustration. His grey eyes sparkled with urgency as he stared at me. "I don't give a damn about the project right now, Amara. People's lives are on the line," he insisted, his voice a mixture of exasperation and concern.

I swallowed hard, feeling a lump form in my throat. He wasn't wrong. We both understood the stakes involved. But I wasn't being irrational either. I had spent too long fighting for this chance.

"Just give me one day," I pleaded, stepping in closer, desperate to bridge the gap between us. "Let's search for them first. If we don't find them by sundown, we'll call for help." My voice trembled, laced with an urgency that belied the fear gnawing at my insides.

His jaw flexed, and I could see the internal struggle warring in him. His shoulders rose and fell dramatically as he took a deep breath. He looked away momentarily, shaking his head as if trying to dispel my words. After what felt like an eternity, he finally sighed in resignation.

"One day," he muttered, his voice tinged with reluctant acceptance. "That's it."

A wave of relief washed over me, but it was fleeting. We both understood the unspoken truth. Time was slipping through our fingers and each moment we hesitated might bring us closer to a reality we both feared.

Chapter Twelve

The morning air was thick with tension as Laken and I stood near the smoldering embers of last night's fire, going back and forth about how to handle the search.

"I'm telling you, we should split up," I insisted, arms crossed tightly over my chest. "It's daylight now, and we'll cover more ground that way."

Laken's expression darkened. "Absolutely not. It's too risky." His voice was sharp, leaving no room for argument. "We don't know what's out there, Amara. You either listen to me, or I'm calling for help. Right now."

My stomach twisted. I knew he meant it. Laken wasn't bluffing, and I couldn't afford to lose his cooperation. Not yet. I swallowed my frustration and forced myself to nod. "Fine. We stay together. But we need a plan."

His stance eased slightly, but his eyes still burned with concern. "We'll start by circling west. That's where Ashten ran. She wouldn't have made it far if she had gotten lost or hurt. After that, we'll loop back northeast toward the homestead."

I hesitated. "You really think Cori went to the homestead?"

Laken exhaled sharply, glancing toward the tree line. "I'm sure. It's the only place that makes sense. If she thought the EMF meter was still out there, she went back for it."

A shiver ran down my spine, but I pushed it aside. I didn't have time for this fear. We needed to be strong for the others and our purpose out here.

"Okay," I said, tightening the straps of my backpack. "Let's go find them."

Before we set off, I approached Wesley, who was nestled beside the flickering fire. Laken had put fresh logs on the red embers, and the flames were beginning to lick at the moss-covered logs. Wesley's eyes were shut, as if he were trying to seek solace in a brief moment of tranquility. Fresh bandages were wrapped around his leg. There was a discernible improvement in his demeanor. I could see his chest's faint rise and fall as he took deep, measured breaths.

I pulled out the note my father had found and my mother's worn, leather-bound notebooks. A familiar ache gripped me as I held them out to him. "Wesley," I said quietly, trying not to let my voice tremble, "can you take these and go through them? See if you can find anything that ties them together. Maybe there's a correlation between what my mom wrote, her note, and what we've experienced."

He gently took them. "Absolutely," he said, his voice calm and reassuring. "I promise you, I'll examine everything thoroughly."

"Thanks," I said, forcing a smile. "If we can find something, maybe we'll understand what we're dealing with out there."

"There's something I need you to do," he said. "If you come across any of our sensors, grab them. I haven't changed them in days. Whatever happened last night..." He didn't need to finish; I understood what he meant. The sensors would have detected them.

"Count on it," I replied.

He gave a slow nod as he flipped through the pages of the battered notebook. His eyes darted over the densely scrawled handwriting that danced in anxious patterns. A frown etched onto his forehead, deepening as he searched for anything that might offer a clue. "I'll let you know if I uncover anything useful," he said, his voice steady. "Just promise me you'll be careful out there, okay?"

I could feel the lump in my throat tightening, rendering me nearly mute. I wanted to assure him I would take every precaution, but the chilling reality loomed larger than our fleeting words. There was no time for soothing sentiments—not when Ashten and Cori were still out there, lost and vulnerable.

Laken, already geared up and ready to go, glanced at me impatiently. "We should move," he said quietly, not wanting to press, but there was urgency in his voice.

I nodded again, lingering for a moment longer, my eyes scanning the forest around us. Then, with one last look at Wesley, I turned away.

Shadows stretched across the forest floor, the golden light of the setting sun barely breaking through the thick canopy. Hours had passed, and my voice was raw from calling their names. The silence that followed each shout made my stomach twist tighter with dread.

"We should stop," Laken said, his voice calm but firm. He stood a few feet ahead of me, his face half-hidden in the growing darkness.

I shook my head, wiping sweat from my forehead. "No. We keep going."

"Amara," he stepped closer, his hands settling on his hips. "It's getting dark."

He could have thrown our deal in my face, but he didn't. The day was over and we were no closer to finding the girls than we had been ten hours ago.

"I don't care!" I snapped, my frustration boiling over. "They're still out here, Laken! We haven't found anything. What if they're hurt? What if they—" My voice broke, and I swallowed down the fear threatening to choke me.

He exhaled sharply, his patience wearing thin. "Listen to me. These girls are smart. If they could, they would've found shelter before nightfall. They wouldn't keep moving in the dark, and neither should we."

I clenched my jaw, my heart pounding with defiance. "So what? We just leave them out here?"

"No, we do what they would have done," he said, stepping closer. His eyes caught what little light remained. "We stop. We rest. And at first light, we pick up the search again. If we keep going now, exhausted and in the dark, we risk getting lost too."

"What about our deal?" I dared to be the one to bring it up.

Laken slid the pack off his back. "You know me, when it comes to you I cave too damn easy." He leaned back against a tree and took a rugged breath. "Which is why I also told Wesley to use the satellite phone in my truck to call for help if we didn't come back by morning, or if they needed help before then, obviously."

I opened my mouth to argue again, but the words wouldn't come. He wasn't wrong, and that infuriated me. Every instinct screamed at me to keep going, but I couldn't ignore the logic in what he was saying. I was supposed to be all about logic.

I exhaled shakily, dragging a hand through my tangled hair. "Fine," I muttered, barely above a whisper. "But we start again at dawn."

Laken nodded. "At dawn."

Reluctantly, I let him lead me toward a small clearing where we could set up for the night. As I sat down, my back against a tree, I kept my ears sharp and listened for any sign of Cori and Ashten in the darkness.

Laken crouched near the fire, carefully stacking small twigs and striking a match. The flames flickered to life. The warmth did little to thaw the cold knot of fear lodged in my chest. All I could picture was Ashten out there shivering and scared. It haunted me every minute.

The distant call of an owl echoed through the trees, its haunting sound sending a fresh wave of worry through me. My eyes burned as I stared into the fire, and the tears came before I could stop myself. They slipped down my cheeks silently, hot against my cool skin.

"Ashten loves owls," I murmured, my voice barely above a whisper.

Laken glanced at me, his expression softening. "Then maybe she'll find comfort in them," he said gently.

I let out a shaky breath, hugging my arms around myself. "She's scared, Laken. She didn't even want to be out here in the first place. And now she's alone. Or worse..." I couldn't bring myself to finish the sentence.

Laken shifted closer, his presence steady. "We don't know that," he said. "Ashten's tough, whether she realizes it or not. She's probably holed up somewhere, waiting for morning. And Cori—" He hesitated. "Cori knew what she was doing when she left camp. She wouldn't have just wandered aimlessly."

I nodded, though the knot in my stomach didn't ease. "I don't know what I'll do if we don't find them, Laken." My voice broke at the end.

He reached out then, hesitating briefly before placing his hand over mine. His touch was warm, reassuring. "We will," he said firmly. "And until then, we stay sharp. We don't give up."

I squeezed my eyes shut, inhaling a trembling breath and finding comfort in his touch. "I just want them to be okay."

Laken tightened his grip on my hand. "Me too."

The owls called again, their voices drifting through the trees like ghostly whispers. I forced myself to listen, to imagine that somehow, wherever she was, Ashten was hearing them too. Maybe she was staring up at the same sky, holding onto hope just like I was.

I let out a hollow, humorless laugh, shaking my head. "You know, I really didn't expect things to go this way."

Laken chuckled dryly beside me, rubbing a hand over his face. "Yeah? What did you expect?"

I gestured vaguely at the dark forest surrounding us. "Certainly not this. I thought we'd set up our equipment, collect some data, maybe get a few creepy recordings that we later analyzed as wildlife." I scoffed. "Never did I picture getting lost in the woods, chased by gawdawful screams, and separated from half our team. This wasn't supposed to turn into the freaking *Blair Witch Project*."

Laken snorted. "Right? Next thing you know, we'll find Ashten standing in a corner somewhere. And just so you know, if that happens, I'm tapping out. I'm done."

I laughed despite myself, though it came out shaky. "Seriously, though, I knew there was something weird about this place, but I didn't think it'd be this bad."

Laken leaned forward, poking at the fire with a stick. "Yeah, well, I won't say I told you so, but the signs were there."

I sighed and tried rubbing some of the tension from my shoulders. "Yeah, well, hindsight's a bitch."

"Your hindsight's a bitch. Mine's fine. I'm just too stupid to acknowledge it and make rash decisions when it comes to you." Our eyes met as he admitted it, and I blushed hard.

We watched the flames flicker and listened to the eerie stillness of the forest. The owls had gone quiet now, leaving only the crackle of the fire and the occasional rustle of leaves in the distance. It was strange how alone we were, but the darkness pushed against us, making it feel suffocating.

Laken exhaled slowly. "Tomorrow, we find them," he said, his voice steady but laced with exhaustion. "No matter what it takes."

I nodded, staring into the fire. "No matter what it takes."

Without a word, Laken reached into his pack and pulled out a thick wool blanket. He shook it out and draped it over us, then leaned back against the fallen log, tugging me gently against his side. I didn't resist. The weight of exhaustion, fear, and the night's events pressed down on me, and for once, I didn't have the energy to fight him.

Above us, the stars peeked through gaps in the branches, shimmering like distant promises. Laken's voice was softer now, barely above a whisper. "You okay?"

I let out a slow breath, my head resting lightly on his shoulder. "No," I admitted. "But I will be."

We lay together beneath the wool blanket, the forest around us strangely quiet. Above, the stars blinked softly through gaps in the branches, distant and unbothered by the chaos below.

"It's almost like the old days," Laken murmured, his voice barely audible above the faint rustling leaves.

I smiled, nostalgia washing over me. "You mean when we'd sneak out to the old barn loft to watch the stars?"

He chuckled, and I felt the gentle vibration through his chest. "Yeah. Back when our biggest worry was getting caught by our parents."

I sighed, closing my eyes as memories came easily. The warm summer nights, whispers beneath wooden beams, while the world felt so far away. "Things were definitely much simpler back then."

Laken shifted closer, his warmth comforting against the chill that had seeped deep into my bones. "They were," he whispered, his voice quieter now, edged with a tenderness I hadn't heard from him in years. "And even then, you always wanted more. You were always chasing something."

I turned my head slightly, looking up into his face. His eyes were soft, illuminated only by the gentle flicker of our dying fire. The look was a gentle reminder of who we'd once been. "Maybe," I admitted. "But I never expected it to lead here."

"Me either," he said, his voice steady but gentle. He paused, as if considering his next words carefully. Finally, he spoke, his voice just a breath. "I missed you, Amara. More than words could ever express."

My chest tightened, emotion swelling in a way I hadn't expected. I opened my mouth to respond, but nothing came out.

Before I could speak, he leaned forward and pressed a soft kiss to my temple. My breath caught, and my eyes fluttered closed. Something inside me melted, the fear and stress momentarily fading into something gentler. I forgot how comforting his arms were.

"Get some rest," he murmured.

I nestled against him. My heart fluttered as I breathed in his familiar scent.

"Goodnight, Laken," I whispered.

"Night, Amara."

As I lay there, encircled in the warm embrace of his strong arms, a deep sense of safety washed over me. The same as it did when we were carefree teenagers. The night sky above us was a canvas of countless stars twinkling like distant diamonds, just as they had done all those years ago. With the cool breeze gently stirring the air, I closed my eyes and surrendered to the sweet comfort of sleep, cocooned in the familiar warmth that felt like home.

CHAPTER THIRTEEN

Wesley

I shifted, wincing as a sharp pain shot through my leg. I gritted my teeth, adjusting the makeshift pillow beneath my head. It was a bundled-up sweatshirt that did little to cushion me from the hard ground. The fire crackled softly, casting flickering shadows across the trees, but its warmth did little to chase away the deep ache settling into my bones.

Tora lay motionless a few feet away, her face pale. Every few minutes, I glanced over at her, reassuring myself that she was still breathing. The quiet of the forest pressed in around me, unnerving in its stillness. I wasn't used to this kind of silence. Back home, there was always some kind of background noise—cars, distant voices, the hum of streetlights. Here, the only sound was the occasional rustling of leaves, the distant call of a bird, and the low pop of burning wood.

I let out a slow breath and shifted again, careful of my injured leg. Laken had done a good job patching me up, but the throbbing pain made it impossible to relax fully. Still, I had a job to do.

Amara had asked me to look through Esme's notes and the cryptic message they'd found. I wasn't sure what I was looking for exactly, but if there was even the slightest chance it could help them understand what was happening, I had to try.

With a grunt, I pushed myself upright, biting back a groan as pain flared through my thigh. I reached for the worn leather journal Amara had given me and flipped it open, the pages crackling with age. The overcast sky illuminated the ink-stained paper, revealing decades of handwritten notes, sketches, and observations.

I sighed, rubbing a hand over my face. "Alright, Esme," I muttered under my breath. "Let's see what you were so afraid of."

Most of Esme's notes are written in shorthand, a mix of scientific observations and personal thoughts. I struggled to decipher some of it, but certain passages stood out. She had been obsessed with the forest's electromagnetic anomalies, recording fluctuations that didn't align with any natural patterns. She mentioned something about energy signatures layering over time, like echoes trapped in space.

I grit my teeth against the pain radiating from my leg and shift slightly, adjusting my position near the dying campfire. Tora still hasn't woken up, her breaths slow but steady. I force myself to focus.

Next, I examine the note Amara's dad found. The words feel ominous, almost like a warning or a curse.

"Those who trespass will lose their way and wander until the forest claims them. And if their blood bleeds true, may they find their damnation."

My brain works through possibilities. Could this be metaphorical? Or was Esme speaking from experience? My gut says it's more than folklore.

I rubbed my forehead, frustration mounting as I flipped through Esme's journals. The pages were covered in notes, scribbled diagrams, half-formed theories, and scattered observations. None of it was straightforward. None of it was clear. I sighed heavily, suddenly questioning why Amara wanted me, of all people, to decipher this.

I was good at numbers and interpreting data. Give me statistics or raw figures, and I could find patterns all day. This was something else entirely. This wasn't data. It was human thought, intuition, fears, and guesses scribbled in haste. It was messy and chaotic. Messy wasn't my specialty.

Why had Amara thought I could do this?

A sharp pang of doubt hit me. What if I missed something critical, something important hidden between the words? I wasn't good with emotion or ambiguity. What if Amara had made a mistake trusting me?

I closed my eyes for a second, forcing myself to take a deep breath. *Stop,* I told myself firmly. *She trusted you for a reason. She knew what she was doing.*

I reopened my eyes, narrowing my focus back on Esme's looping handwriting. Amara didn't need perfection, just another perspective. I was the objective who didn't have their emotions tangled up in the history of Oak Hollow. I could do this.

With renewed determination, I picked a journal back up and refocused my attention. If there was something hidden here, a connection Amara hadn't seen, I'd find it. Numbers or not, I wasn't about to let her down.

One entry caught my attention. It was dated just a few days before Esme disappeared, which is different from the rest. The handwriting is shaky, hurried.

"*I finally understand. The forest doesn't just react, it remembers. And it doesn't forget. If I don't come back, tell Amara to be careful. I know she's determined to prove me wrong, but some things should never be disturbed.*"

I swallowed hard. Whatever Esme was onto, she was afraid of it.

I flipped through the fragile pages, my eyes scanning Esme's looping handwriting. My fingers lingered on another entry dated nearly two decades ago. The ink was slightly smudged.

"*April 3rd, Lana Jacobs came to me today. Said she barely made it out. That the trees moved when she wasn't looking, twisting the path back on itself. She swears she walked in a straight line, but somehow ended up right where she started. She also claimed something whispered her name, just out of sight. She was convinced that if she had stayed any longer, she would've disappeared like the others.*"

I exhaled, flipping to another entry, this one older.

"*November 12th, Peter Crane was found wandering outside the forest's edge. He had been missing for three days. His eyes were wild, unfocused. He spoke in fragmented sentences, repeating over and over that he 'lost time.' He couldn't recall how he survived, only that the sun never rose. He kept muttering about shadows that weren't his own."*

A chill crept up my spine as I skimmed more accounts—stories of people hearing their own voices calling from the trees, of figures standing just beyond the firelight, of sudden disorientation that left even experienced hikers lost for hours.

Then came the theories.

Esme had been meticulous in documenting them. Some aligned with folklore, such as spirits of the wrongfully buried or nature reclaiming those who trespassed. Others were more scientific. She wrote about the possibility of geomagnetic anomalies disrupting perception, causing vivid hallucinations. She suggested that something, whether natural or supernatural, fed off human energy, draining them, confusing them, and making them vulnerable.

I leaned closer to the fire, rubbing my aching leg. The bandages Laken had wrapped held firm, but pain throbbed deep in the muscle. I gritted my teeth and turned another page.

Esme's notes were becoming more frantic the further I read. Her careful, scientific observations gradually gave way to something more desperate. It teetered with obsession.

"I have felt it now. The pull. It knows me. It knows my blood."

"The whispers are clearer at the homestead. They know my name."

"If I go further, will I understand? Or will I be lost like the others?"

I swallowed hard. The handwriting in the last few entries was jagged, almost erratic. I glanced toward Tora, still unconscious beneath the blanket they'd placed over her. The fire crackled, but beyond its glow, the trees loomed dark and impenetrable.

I looked back at the notebook, flipping forward to where I had tucked a loose page inside. It was the note Amara's father had found. I traced the words with my fingers, reading them aloud under my breath.

"Those who trespass will lose their way and wander until the forest claims them. And if their blood bleeds true, may they find their damnation."

My stomach tensed. I had heard folklore before, superstitions meant to keep people from wandering too far into places they didn't belong. This felt different. The way Esme wrote about the forest, she hadn't just studied it. She had been afraid of it.

A sudden gust of wind pushed through camp, sending embers spiraling up toward the sky. I stiffened. The trees groaned softly in response, their limbs creaking in protest.

A soft groan pulled my attention away from Esme's journal. My head snapped up, and I looked over to see Tora stirring on her sleeping pad, her face pale beneath tangled strands of hair.

"Tora?" I said quietly, setting the notebook aside and shifting carefully toward her.

She blinked slowly and pressed a hand to her forehead, wincing. "God, my head feels like it's splitting open." Her eyes finally found mine, confusion clouding them. "What happened?"

I hesitated, unsure how much she remembered or how much she'd even believe. "You don't remember anything?" I asked softly.

She shook her head slightly, still squinting against the pain. "Just fragments. Walking through the forest. Darkness." She shuddered, pulling the blanket tighter around herself. "After that, nothing." Her voice trembled slightly as she looked up at me, searching my face. "Why do I feel like I got hit by a truck?" She then noticed my leg. "And what happened to you?"

I exhaled slowly, choosing my words carefully. "We were in the woods looking for Cori. You and I got separated when I fell down a ravine and got hurt. You came after me, and then the screams started. They disoriented both of us."

Tora's brow furrowed deeply, skepticism flickering in her eyes. "Screams?" She forced a strained laugh. "Are you sure you didn't hit your head too?"

I met her eyes steadily. "I wish I were making it up." I paused again, my mouth dry. "When Amara and Laken found us... You were..." I hesitated, searching for the gentlest way to explain, "You were suspended in the air. Like someone was holding you up, but there was nobody there."

Her eyes widened, fear and disbelief warring on her face. "Suspended? What, like a doll?" she scoffed, shaking her head again, harder now. "That's impossible."

"I know," I said quietly. "But I saw it. Amara saw it. Laken saw it. It was real."

She stared at me for a long, tense moment, clearly torn between rejecting my words and confronting the raw fear now creeping into her expression. Her voice lowered to a whisper as she looked away. "How is this even happening? We were supposed to be here for a damn school assignment, Wes. Not being tormented by something that shouldn't even exist, if it does." She rubbed at her temple again, visibly shaken. "How do we know it's not just some crazy local finding humor in our fear?"

"We don't," I admitted softly, though explaining what happened to her being a human prank was far-fetched. "Everything in Esme's journal and everything we've experienced points to something more than just some hoax. I can't explain it yet, but I'm determined to try."

She fell silent and stared into the fire as the weight of what I'd said settled over her. Finally, she spoke again, her voice steadier. "Then we get to work. Whatever's happening can't win. Not if we have anything to do with it."

I nodded firmly, even though uncertainty still gripped my chest. "Damn straight."

I winced as Tora tightened the fresh bandage around my leg. A line of cursed phrases ran through my mind as I stared up into the darkening sky. I'd kill for some painkiller right about now.

"You're lucky," she muttered, her brows knit together in concentration. "A little to the right and you'd be in real trouble." So I've been told.

"Yeah, I feel super lucky right now," I said dryly, shifting on the makeshift cot Tora set up for me. My muscles ached, and my head felt heavy, but at least the throbbing in my leg had dulled a little.

Tora sighed and stood, brushing her hands off on her jeans. "I made some food. You need to eat." She handed me a steaming plate of beans and rice. It was simple, but it smelled good, and I hadn't realized how hungry I was until now.

"Do you think they'll find them?" Tora finally asked, her voice small.

I hesitated. I knew she wanted reassurance, but I wasn't sure what to say. "I hope so," I admitted. "But something about all of this isn't normal."

Tora let out a short, bitter laugh. "No kidding." She poked at her food with her fork. "I keep thinking about it all. Ashten, being so terrified, she ran into the dark alone. And where the hell is Cori?"

I exhaled through my nose, gripping the notebook in my lap. "Esme was scared too," I murmured, flipping back through her notes. "She knew something was wrong with this place. She documented years of weird experiences, and yet she kept coming back. Like she had to figure it out, no matter what."

Tora frowned. "And look what happened to her."

A heavy silence settled between us. Esme's outcome was all too real a possibility for any of them. The thought of losing one of my friends, let alone my own life, was terrifying. The fire popped, causing me to flinch.

"We should have called for help," Tora whispered.

I didn't answer because deep down, I agreed with Amara. If we could keep fighting a little longer, we could uncover something no one else had. But keeping the secret of Laken's satellite phone from Tora was a sharp burden. It was one I would keep letting poke at me until I could no longer take its edges.

I shifted on the cot to find a position that didn't send a sharp jolt of pain through my leg. The fire's warmth barely reached me, and the distant hoots of owls echoed through the trees, reminding me how deep we were in the middle of nowhere. I exhaled slowly, forcing myself to relax. If I didn't get rest, I wouldn't be any good to anyone.

Tora sat nearby, her fingers absentmindedly twisting the hem of her jacket. I wanted to say something to reassure her that everything was going to be fine, but exhaustion pulled at me too hard. I let my heavy eyelids close, surrendering to sleep.

The moment I drifted into the darkness, it was as if something pulled me somewhere else entirely.

The fire was gone. The forest was silent as I stood in the middle of it. The trees loomed taller, their twisted branches curling toward me. A thick mist rolled over the ground, swirling around my feet.

A whisper drifted through the air, distant but unmistakable.

"Wesley."

My breath hitched, and I turned in circles, searching for the source. The trees appeared to stretch endlessly in every direction, identical and suffocating. My pulse quickened.

"Those who trespass will lose their way and wander until the forest claims them."

Esme's words hung in the air, no longer just ink sprawled across a page, but vibrant and alive. They swirled around me, each phrase a twisted vine that threatened to ensnare me in their grip. The gravity of her voice seemed to push against me, as if the very essence of her words could reach out and pull me under. Her thoughts, once neatly organized in my mind, now spilled forth in a chaotic torrent demanding my attention.

"Help me."

A dark shadow flitted between the gnarled trunks of towering trees, each one draped in a tangle of creeping vines and thick moss. My heart raced as I strained to pinpoint the shape that slipped through the underbrush. My breath quickened, and the chill in the air sent shivers down my spine. Each time I thought I had captured its outline, it evaporated into the shadows. Its presence was more palpable and unsettling.

The forest around me felt alive, the rustling leaves whispering secrets while the scent of damp earth filled my lungs. I squinted against the dimness, every nerve in my body on alert, but the figure danced effortlessly through the trees.

A sharp scream pierced the air.

"...find their damnation."

Each word was full of agony. It ripped through the silence, shaking the trees. I clapped my hands over my ears, but it did nothing to stop the sound. It grew louder, rising to an unbearable pitch until—

I gasped awake, my body jerking violently.

Tora rushed to my side. "Wesley? What's wrong?"

I wiped the sweat from my face, chest heaving. I could still hear the echo of the words in my ears, still feel the weight of that voice in the depths of my mind.

"Nothing," I lied, my voice hoarse. "Just a bad dream." Tora was already worried. There was no need to make things worse over a nightmare.

As I lay back against the pillow, I couldn't help but rethink the dream. The agony. While Esme had written the words, she wasn't the original author. Whoever it was had suffered a great deal. The question was, what?

Chapter Fourteen

Malva Thaine, 1876

I once lived peacefully among the towering oaks. Our land was a haven of tranquility, lush and green. It was the kind of place where, if you pressed your ear to the earth, you could feel it vibrating softly with life. The expansive forest cradled our small farm on three sides, creating a natural barrier.

In this secluded spot, I served as the local healer, a role filled with both respect and suspicion. Though many sought my assistance, some would whisper "witch" behind closed shutters. My husband, Eben, always stood by my side, calling me blessed by the earth. He passed away five winters ago, leaving a void that echoed throughout our home. He was laid to rest in the family plot, a serene spot beneath a moss-covered cross. Since his departure, it has been just me, our daughter, the fertile land, and the whispering forest surrounding us.

I had grown deeply attuned to the rhythms of nature—the subtle cadence of the seasons and the myriad voices that filled the woods. I could identify which roots to boil for fever relief and which leaves to steep for a calming sleep. I recognized each animal by its distinctive sounds, the rustle of leaves signaling their movements. I understood the trees by their moods. They swayed in the breeze and stood rigid against a storm. The old oaks, especially, spoke to me with an ancient wisdom. Their gnarled branches and thick trunks resonated with the stories of the land.

However, something was changing. An unsettling shift rippled through the air, disturbing the delicate balance I had come to know so well.

It began with an eerie silence that blanketed the landscape. The once vibrant melodies of chirping birds faded into an unsettling hush. The graceful deer that typically roamed the edges of the forest vanished from sight. Even the wind seemed still, holding its breath as if aware of the impending gloom.

Then came the dreams. They were dark and twisted specters that invaded my nights. These were not mere figments of imagination but vivid narratives filled with shadowy figures whispering secrets within the confines of an ancient forest. Trees bled an inky black substance, their bark gnarled and twisted.

Initially, I dismissed these visions as the product of my own grief and loneliness. It was a way for my mind to process the silence around me. Yet as the nights passed, the dreams became more lifelike. Each image dripped with a sense of foreboding that was impossible to ignore.

As the sun rose each morning, trouble began to seep into the town like a slow poison. Whispers were exchanged, then morphed into rumors that danced through the streets like a wildfire. The faces of the townsfolk grew tight with fear. Fear was a palpable force that twisted the air.

My daughter, Elowen, was seventeen. She was a radiant beacon of kindness in a world often darkened with terror. Possessing a brilliance that surpassed her years, she inherited her father's steady hands, skilled at crafting and mending. She also had my gift for listening. With patience and grace, she tutored the valley's children. She awakened their minds to the wonders of reading, writing, and critical thinking. Parents couldn't help but praise her gentleness.

But when misfortune struck and illness swept through the valley like a shadow, the tide of admiration quickly turned. The children began to fall ill. Their once vibrant faces faded into paleness, and the laughter that echoed in the valley grew silent, just like it had in the forest.

In their desperation to find someone to blame, the villagers first turned their eyes upon me. They whispered in hushed tones, accusing me of failing to heal the fragile lives entrusted to my care. When one child managed to survive my treatment, they quickly shifted their focus away from me to Elowen. She was the one who spent the most time nurturing and guiding their young children.

The whispering and blame grew. They claimed she had poisoned the children's veins with dark magic and her nurturing lessons were nothing more than sinister incantations designed to taint their children's minds. Their once thankful spirits twisted into something grotesque with fear. None of what they said was true. Truth was often lost and overshadowed by suspicion and dread.

In the dead of night, a mob descended upon our home, a group of neighbors I had once cared for during their fevered nights and the painful groans of childbirth. Where there had been camaraderie, now there was only chaos. Their faces were twisted by collective hysteria as they stormed through the front door. I could only watch in horror as they seized Elowen from her bed. Her frightened cries echoed in the stillness of the night. I pleaded with them to see reason, but my words fell on deaf ears.

With cruel hands, they bound her to a weather-worn post just beyond the edge of the woods. The trees stood watch, their branches stretched toward the heavens, bearing witness to this inexcusable betrayal. There, on that boundary between the safety of home and the foreboding forest, she became a sacrifice to extinguish their fears. I felt the icy grip of despair tighten around my heart as the world around us descended into madness.

They said she would feel the pain she inflicted on others. That fire would purify her soul.

As her screams echoed through the valley, the wind rose. The trees twisted, groaned, and shuddered in fury. The fire leapt higher than it should have. The sky darkened, though it was still night. The stars vanishing from sight.

I fell to my knees and did not weep. Devastation hollowed me out. I no longer felt the sun's warmth or the comfort of birdsong. I no longer believed in mercy.

They took everything from me. My child, my peace, my place in the world was gone.

Let it be known, it was not madness that took root and drove my actions. It was justice.

I waited two moons in silence, letting their guilt ferment and letting the whispers grow in the dark corners of their minds. Then, in the hush before the harvest, I took what they cherished most. One of their own daughters.

She was young and innocent, just as my Elowen had been. I did not take her to punish her. I took her because her blood was theirs. Because the forest does not ask for kindness. It asks for balance.

I led her to the old grove, a sacred enclave where the roots entwine in an intricate dance deep beneath the earth. The air was thick with the scent of damp earth and decaying leaves. Towering ancient oaks stood tall around us.

Here, in this sacred place, I would make my own offering. My blood and hers would mingle with the soil of the earth to always remember. I drew the blade across my palm, the sharp sting a welcome distraction from the turmoil within.

This act was not born of fury. It was a testament to the grief that engulfed my heart. Every drop that fell seemed to whisper the stories of loss and longing, echoing through the roots and into the earth. It was binding my sorrow to the very fabric of this grove.

I softly murmured the incantation, my voice barely rising above the chilling howl of the wind that swept through the night. It was a moment suspended in time, where nature and emotion intertwined, both filled with longing and despair.

"Those who trespass will lose their way and wander until the forest claims them. And if their blood bleeds true, may they find their damnation."

It was neither a scream nor a desperate prayer cast into the void. It was a curse—raw and potent, laced with the bitterness of a heart scorned.

From that fateful day onward, Oak Hollow transformed. What had once been a serene haven was no longer merely a tranquil retreat from the world. It took on a new essence, becoming sacred yet cursed, a place imbued with both reverence and dread.

Chapter Fifteen

Wesley

I woke with a jolt, a strangled gasp catching in my throat. My hand instinctively gripped my thigh, the pain sharp and real. Nothing compared to the terror clawing its way through my chest. My heart thundered like it was trying to escape my ribcage, and for a moment, I couldn't tell where I was.

The fire had burned low, casting the camp in a low orange glow. The dream clung to me like smoke. The woman. The fire. Her voice was like wind in the leaves. Her curse whispered into the bones of the forest.

"Those who trespass will lose their way..."

I sat up too fast and winced as the pain in my leg flared again, but I forced myself through it. I reached for Esme's journal, flipping through the pages with shaking hands. There it was again. Written more than once in Esme's spidery handwriting.

"Those who trespass will lose their way..."

She had been tracking the words not just as a superstition or campfire legend. She'd been connecting it to a timeline. A woman. A curse.

Malva Thaine.

I remembered the name now. It had been buried in one of Esme's earlier entries.

"Malva Thaine, widow, healer. Her daughter, Elowen, was executed after being blamed for a string of child deaths. Malva vanished shortly after, and the disappearances began within months."

My hands trembled as I connected the final thread. Malva hadn't vanished. She had become part of the forest. The strange behavior of the forest, the screams, the hallucinations, the way it seemed to know us, all made sense now. The curse.

This wasn't just bad energy or magnetic interference. This wasn't just folklore. This was personal. A land soaked in blood. A curse etched into the roots. A forest that remembered.

I glanced over at Tora, deep in a peaceful sleep. She was completely unaware of the turmoil swirling in my mind. I had gathered all the evidence, yet it felt surreal. Every piece of information seemed to contradict reason, yet here it was, hauntingly real.

It wasn't random. It never had been.

My thoughts raced as I flipped through Esme's later entries, finally understanding what I hadn't before. Her obsession with the forest, her desperate need to document everything, and her warnings hidden among lines of scientific data revealed a deeper truth. She wasn't just studying Oak Hollow; she was bound to it. She was a descendant of its history.

Esme hadn't just been curious; the forest had called to her. It had recognized her. She had delved deep into the lore to protect her own. Esme understood the dangers of lingering too far into the forest but felt compelled to do so. She sought to uncover and stop the curse to save Amara.

"Oh God." My voice came out broken, barely audible over the dying fire.

Amara was out there, deep in the woods. The blood of Malva Thaine coursed through the forest's veins, and Amara was tethered to the same cursed land that had swallowed her mother. She believed this was about research, about finishing what Esme had started, but it was far more personal than that.

If the curse held true, the forest was waiting for her.

I scrambled for my makeshift crutch, pain forgotten in the rush of adrenaline. I had to do something quick. If we didn't do something soon, Oak Hollow wouldn't let Amara return.

Chapter Sixteen

Amara

I stirred awake slowly, as if rising from the depths of a dream that lingered just out of reach. The soft glow of morning light trickled through the lush branches above, creating a mosaic of warmth and shadows across the dewy grass beneath us.

Blinking against the brightness, I gazed up at the intricate canopy, where vibrant greens merged with hints of browns and yellows. My mind felt heavy and clouded. An unsettling fog wrapped around my thoughts and I found myself disoriented. I struggled to piece together the fragments of where I was and what had led me to this tranquil yet unsettling place. The weight that pressed down on me was both physical and emotional. It was as if the very earth beneath me was urging me to remember something I couldn't.

Beside me, Laken stirred.

He sat up, rubbing a hand across his face, squinting at the soft light filtering through the trees. His expression twisted with confusion. "Where are we?"

I pushed myself up, the wool blanket slipping off my shoulders. "What do you mean?"

He turned in a slow circle, eyes scanning the surrounding woods like he was seeing them for the first time. "I don't remember setting up camp here."

I froze. I didn't either.

The fire pit was nothing but cold ash. The trees surrounding us were dense and unfamiliar. My stomach tightened as a strange sense of wrongness settled over me.

"We were supposed to…" I trailed off, the words sticking in my throat. What were we supposed to do?

Laken frowned, his brow furrowing. "I feel like we should be doing something."

I nodded slowly. "Me too. But I can't remember what."

We stared into the woods like the answer might be hiding from us. It was like we'd woken from one dream into another. Except in this dream, it was as if something important had been taken from us while we slept. Something we should've remembered.

Laken stood slowly, brushing leaves from his jeans. "We can't just sit here. We need to find our way out." Pulling out his phone, he opened his compass app. He walked in a circle once more. Suddenly, he stopped, then pointed west, toward a path barely visible between the trees. "We should head that way," he said, his voice quiet but certain. "If I'm right, an old homestead is west of here. From there, we can get our bearings. Maybe even find our way out."

I stared at him, still trying to shake the thick fog in my head. "You remember that, but not how we got here or why?" Not knowing was the worst feeling ever. A flash of anxiety swarmed my senses.

He hesitated, then shrugged. "I guess it's like muscle memory. My head's fuzzy, but I know that direction leads somewhere familiar."

The homestead. The word alone made my skin crawl, though I didn't know why. I had a faint memory of that place, but again, the how eluded me. Still, Laken's logic made sense. We needed a landmark. I could handle logic.

"Okay," I said slowly, pushing myself to my feet. "I trust you."

We gathered our things in silence, though strangely, I couldn't remember unpacking anything. The blanket was here, my flashlight, my pack. It was all laid out neatly like we'd planned this. I didn't remember doing any of it.

I followed Laken west, the trees looming around us like guards. The forest felt tighter somehow, closer. The further we went, the more something in me tugged forward. Not by memory, but by something else I couldn't explain.

Finally, the forest gave way to a clearing with such unexpected abruptness that it felt as though we had stepped through a veil. We paused at the boundary, the towering trees behind us looming. It was as if we were standing between two separate worlds.

Before us stretched the remnants of an old homestead. The blackened timbers were charred and bore silent witness to the ravages of time and nature. Moss crept over the stones, cloaking them in a velvety green shroud, while warped beams jutted awkwardly from the earth like broken ribs of a forgotten home. The air was thick with the scent of damp earth and decay.

An unsettling feeling crept through my veins as I took it all in.

The trees here were wrong. They were twisted and gnarled, their bark scorched in places, their limbs bare despite the season. The wind didn't whisper here. It howled. Beneath the wind, there were screams, or what I perceived as such. They were low but were carried through the hollows like echoes from a nightmare.

What happened here?

Laken stood beside me; his eyes locked on the ruins of the home. "Do you feel that?"

I didn't answer. My breath was shallow. Panic was swelling like a tide. My eyes darted around the clearing, landing on every shattered remnant of the house and every shadow that seemed to stretch too far.

Then a memory. It whispered to me with a gentleness that didn't fit this place.

This is where my mother died.

My knees went weak as a sharp breath left my lungs.

Laken looked at me, confusion deepening into concern. "Amara?"

I turned in a slow circle, my vision blurring with tears and dread as more memories began to surface. The fear we'd felt hours ago. "Cori," I choked. "Ashten." My voice cracked with their names. Something about saying them aloud cut through the thick fog that had settled over us.

Beside me, Laken staggered, his eyes wide. His hand reached out to steady himself against one of the crooked limbs of a tree. His fingers curled around the weathered wood. His neutral expression cracked. Fear replaced it.

"I can't believe it," he murmured. "The survivors... they weren't lying." He ran a hand down his face as he tried wrapping his mind around it all. "Could that be what the note meant?"

Laken was rambling, and I wasn't putting together what he meant. "What are you talking about?"

"The people who survive," he continued, almost in a whisper. "They never remember. They're the ones who don't have ties to this place. The ones who don't bleed true."

I falter for a minute. His reasoning was sound. It also made sense why some survived and some were never found. A shiver rippled down my spine, cold and sharp. Still, I wasn't sure I believed it. The wind howled differently here because of the gnarled trees and cracked branches. As for the moment of haze, perhaps there was a poisonous fungus in the part of the forest where we slept. We wouldn't know until we tested it.

Looking at Laken, I decided to hold my argument. There was no point to it now. Plus, Ashten and Cori were still out there. "What do we need to do now, Laken?"

Laken turned back toward the burned-out frame of the house. His gaze scanned what remained of the foundation. His eyes narrowed with intent. "The EMF meter," he said suddenly.

I blinked, caught off guard. That was not what I had been expecting. "What?"

"Your mother's EMF meter. It was never recovered after she disappeared, right?"

He started digging through the rubble. "If there's any device out here sensitive enough to track whatever this place is doing, it's that meter. Your mom built it for this forest. For its energy. She knew more than she ever put in those reports."

How was something like that even possible? Could someone cue a design specific to something like that? Perhaps with the right anomalies. It was something I would have to bring to Wesley's attention.

My eyes swept across the ruins. "You think it's still here?"

"If it is," he said, "we need to find it. It might be the only thing that can help us see what we can't." Made sense.

We picked our way through the remnants of the homestead. My hands were stained black from the ash and charred beams I dug around. Laken's face had streaks of dirt from where he wiped away the sweat.

Feeling as if we had overturned every stone and found nothing, I moved toward what was left of the barn. The structure was leaning dangerously to one side, with one corner of the roof collapsed entirely. Vines had overtaken most of it, and rusted tools hung on what was left of the back wall.

I stepped carefully between two boards, my boots crunching over brittle debris.

"Be careful," Laken called. He was still digging through the remnants of the house. "That thing's not exactly OSHA approved."

"Noted," I muttered, sweeping my flashlight across the interior.

The beam of my flashlight sliced through the thick veil of dust and shadow, illuminating a world of forgotten boards, tangled ropes, and a cracked jar spilling its rusty nails. Stepping deeper inside, I swept the light methodically from one corner to the other.

Then something flickered at the edge of my vision, a sudden movement in the far corner catching the light on my third sweep. I approached cautiously, compelled to see what was huddled beneath the sagging hayloft.

My breath hitched as I froze. It was a person, wreathed in layers of grime and cocooned in a tattered jacket that hung loosely around her frail form. My heart raced, each thud echoing in my ears.

"Ashten?" I breathed, my voice barely rising above a whisper.

At the sound of my voice, she flinched but slowly lifted her head. Her eyes were haunted.

"Ashten," I gasped, urgency propelling me forward. "Oh my god!"

As I hurried to her side, she collapsed forward. "Amara," she sobbed, the sound a heart-wrenching whisper that cut through the stillness.

Dropping to my knees in the dirt, I enveloped her in my arms. She trembled against my chest. "I've got you," I murmured soothingly. "You're okay. You're safe now."

Laken appeared in the doorway, his breath catching sharply as his shocked gaze fell upon her. "Is she—?" he started, uncertainty threading his voice.

"She's alive," I replied, the rawness of my emotions surfacing as I held Ashten tightly, my relief palpable in the trembling silence.

Chapter Seventeen

Cori

I stumbled through the forest, my breath sharp and ragged in my chest. My arms are scraped from the briars, and the taste of copper clung to the back of my throat. My legs burned, pleading for me to stop, but I wouldn't. I didn't know how long I'd been walking, but I had to keep going. Time didn't work right in this place.

No matter what Amara or her scientist friends believe, these woods are haunted. I'd seen too much not to believe it. I heard the voices. They were too soft to catch the words, but too clear to be my imagination. I felt the air shift around me when there was no wind.

The first time I came out here with Esme and Laken, I thought I was just scared. My mind was playing with my fear. Then, I learned the truth. It wasn't my mind playing with me; it was the forest. It knows how to play tricks. It knows how to feed off your fear, and it does.

My foot caught on a root and I fell hard. My palms scrape raw against the dirt, the sting causing me to wince. I lay there for a second, too tired to move. My eyes burned with hot, frustrated tears.

I wanted to be strong. I wanted to prove that I wasn't afraid of this place. I always hated how Esme wouldn't let me tag along. It was as if she didn't trust me. Now, I wonder if she was only trying to protect me.

The past few days have taught me that. No amount of logic or bravado can explain what I've seen. I've watched the same shadow pass between the trees three times. I've heard laughter when there was no one there to laugh. Then, there was the woman. She was pale and silent, always standing out of the length of the light. When I blinked, she would disappear.

I rolled onto my back and stared up through the tangle of branches above me. Only a few slivers of sunlight reached me, and even those felt cold.

This forest wasn't just a place. It was a being that never wanted to let you go.

I blinked, sure I'd only fallen asleep for a minute, but the sun was lower. It would be dark again soon.

My heart sank. The weight of despair wrapped around me, heavy and suffocating. The forest was like an insatiable predator, ready to swallow me whole. I was exhausted, teetering on the edge of surrender. I didn't want to face another night steeped in fear.

A single tear slipped down my cheek, carving a path through the grime that clung to my skin. The wind began to pick up, setting the leaves into a frantic dance and carrying with it a new scent of hope. Smoke.

I froze, the forest fading as I lifted my head and breathed deeply. The aroma filled my lungs, delicate yet unmistakable. It mingled with the damp, earthy notes of moss and decaying leaves. Someone had to be nearby.

Drawing from the well of adrenaline surging through my veins, I pushed myself upright. My legs trembled and protested with every movement. I clawed at the rough bark of trees and grabbed hold of branches to steady myself. My instincts guided me, my nose leading the way like a compass.

As I trudged onward, the forest underwent a subtle transformation. It no longer felt like a labyrinth meant to disorient me; it seemed to shift and guide me. The trees parted in an almost inviting manner. The path ahead unfolded clearly, with each step drawing me closer to the promise of safety.

Breaking through the final barrier of trees, I stumbled into a clearing. The remnants of the fire pit lay before me, still smoldering softly. Ribbons of smoke curled lazily into the twilight sky. My heart leapt at the familiar sight.

"Wesley?"

He jerked upright from where he'd been dozing beside the fire. His face was pale and drawn, but his expression shattered with relief when he saw me.

"Cori!"

I barely made it a few more steps before I collapsed next to him. The warmth from the flames offered comfort, though it didn't quite reach the chill deep in my bones. I wrapped my arms around myself, shivering uncontrollably as Tora looked up at the commotion. Seeing me, she instinctively started moving. I was thankful for the blanket she wrapped around my shoulders.

She then started moving quietly around the camp with a spoon in hand. My stomach growled painfully, louder than I cared to admit. I hadn't realized how hungry I was until the thought of food became a possibility. But even as my stomach twisted in need, I couldn't shake the deep chill that had settled in me. It wasn't that cold outside. The air was crisp, but not chilling. Still, I felt like I was freezing from the inside out. It was like something had grabbed hold of me, deep in my gut, and wouldn't let go.

Wesley's voice broke through my foggy thoughts. "I'm so glad you made it back," he said softly, his eyes fixed on me. His face was gaunt, the weariness of the last few days etched into his features. He hadn't looked this tired when I left.

I nodded, trying to smile, but the motion felt foreign. "I don't even know how I made it."

Tora set a bowl of food down in front of me, and I gratefully took it. The food's warmth soothed me, but it did nothing for the heaviness in my chest. "Where is everyone else?"

Wesley shifted closer, his voice a little quieter now. "They're still out there." He looked to the forest. "Amara and Laken went looking for you and Ashten."

I should have known they would. "When did they leave?"

"Yesterday." Wesley wet his lips, seeming uncomfortable with what he was about to say. He rubbed a hand over his face, looking exhausted. "Cori, this place... It's nothing like I've experienced before. I always debunked things like this as nonsense." He shook his head, still not fully trusting what he was saying. "I don't know that I can say that anymore."

My spoon clanked against the bowl as I set it aside. I could relate to this feeling all too well. "I know what you mean," I whispered. "I used to be skeptical, too. This place made me a believer at too early of an age." A shiver ran down my spine thinking about it.

"What happened?" Wesley asked, then hurried to add, "If you don't mind me asking."

I didn't. Some people don't like to talk about their painful past, others do. I am one of those people. It's how I've healed. "When I was twelve, my cousin from California came to visit. My aunt and uncle own and tend a grape farm, so she's no stranger to the outdoors. We decided we wanted to go camping as she hadn't been in years, but my parents were too busy. Adulting, I get it now."

Wesley snorted at that. "No lie there."

"Anyway, they got my older brother to take us for a few days. On the second night, I woke up and she was gone." Tears stung the back of my eyes, and my throat began to burn as I tried holding back my emotions. "Days went by, and we couldn't find her. It was so scary. Then, one day, she's found at the edge of the Thaine Homestead. When they carried her out of the forest and our eyes met, I knew she wasn't the same."

Wesley's eyes softened. "What happened to her?"

"She ended up in a mental health hospital." I swallowed hard, hating how it all ended. "She's still there today. She never recovered."

"That's terrible. I'm so sorry." Wesley looked away from me, seemingly lost for words.

I mentally slap myself when I think back to how we got on this topic. Wesley had wanted to admit his own defeats, not listen to mine.

"Anyway, enough about how I got suckered into the tale that is Oak Hollow. What were you saying?"

He seemed to refocus and shifts uneasily in his chair. "You're not the only one who's seen things and lived to tell about them." He took a deep breath. "Esme witnessed a lot, and thankfully, she wrote it all down. She knew something unprecedented was happening. The cursed land, the disappearances, and how the forest changes people."

I met his eyes, the weight of his words pressing down on me. "How do you know all this?"

Wesley's voice softened, the tremor in his words betraying his calm demeanor. "I've been reading her journals and piecing them together. The forest is cursed, Cori. And I think it wants Amara."

There didn't seem to be a reason as to who it chose and who it didn't. "What makes you think it's Amara?" There were three of them still out there. It could take Laken or Ashten just the same. It could take them all.

"I've been going through Esme's journal," he continued. "And comparing it to the note Amara's dad found."

"What note?"

"Sorry. I forgot you weren't here for that." He leaned forward and rifled through his bag. The piece of paper he pulls out is worn with age. He hands it to me. "Amara thought it was some kind of warning. It's not. It's a curse."

As I read the words, I quivered. This answered so much but opened the door to more. "How can you be sure?"

"Last night, I had a dream. Well, I'd call it a nightmare considering how real it felt. It was like someone was showing me their life through their eyes."

That got my attention.

He leaned closer, his voice lowering as the fire crackled. "There was a woman. Her name was Malva Thaine. She lived out here in the late 1800s. She was a healer. What I imagine we call a nurse today. Anyway, her husband died and she became a widow. Tragedy struck again when her daughter was falsely accused of murdering children and burned alive. The pain from all of that changed Malva. She turned to the forest for revenge."

"The curse," I whispered, already putting the pieces together. "Being a healer and knowing how to use the land, it would make sense for her to turn to it for comfort." As terrible as it is, and what everyone has been through, I couldn't say that I blamed her. My heart broke for her.

Wesley continued. "She decided she was going to take one of theirs. So, she took the mayor's daughter and spilled her blood, along with her own, onto the land. As she's doing this, she speaks the curse. *Those who trespass will lose their way.* That's why so many become confused and lost."

I looked down at the paper. "*But if their blood bleeds true, may they find their damnation.*" The forest suddenly felt closer as if it was holding its breath and listening. I swallowed hard. "And Amara's tied to it because of Esme."

"Because of their blood," Wesley said. "They're descendants of the town. That's why the forest wants them. It didn't take me or Tora. It didn't take you. It took Esme. And now it's calling to Amara."

My stomach twisted. I always believed something strange and unexplainable was happening in Oak Hollow. To hear its truth seems unimaginable.

Wesley then started talking about heading out to search for them. He thought if we retraced my steps, we could eventually run into them. I shook my head, hard.

"No," I said firmly. "It would be reckless for us to go after them."

He blinked at me like my words were foreign. "What are you talking about? We just learned—"

"I know what we learned, Wesley, but think about it." I sat forward, setting my bowl aside, no longer able to even think about swallowing another bite. "It would be like running around blindfolded, playing *Marco Polo* in a forest that changes its own damn rules. We could get lost all over again."

He opened his mouth to argue, but I pressed on. "You can't even walk. I'm running on fumes. Tora is not going alone. If we go out there again without a plan, injured, and completely exhausted, we might not return. Again!"

Wesley tensed his jaw, causing his dark skin to flex over his facial muscles. Then he let out a long breath and nodded reluctantly. "You're right," he said softly. "But we can't just sit here and wait."

A new plan formed in my mind. Amara would kill me for what I was about to do, but I didn't care. We were out of time and needed to find them.

I stood, my legs still sore and stiff, but steady enough. "There's only one person who can help us now," I said, grabbing my jacket and turning toward the edge of camp.

Wesley looked up at me, confused. "What are you talking about? Who?"

I paused just long enough to meet his eyes. "Amara's dad."

He blinked, stunned. "What? Cori, no! Amara specifically didn't want him involved. She said—"

"I know what she said," I cut in, grabbing my flashlight. "But we've got missing people and a forest that appears cursed. Her dad has more experience with these woods than any of us. He's the only one who might know how to find her. More importantly, how to bring her back."

Wesley stood, wincing from the pain in his leg. "Fine, but we are coming with you. I have questions, and maybe he can help figure them out, too."

"I'm going to stay here," Tora said, having sat quietly while Wesley and I had been combating stories and ideas. Tora was quiet, but smart. Or so I thought.

"You don't need to stay here by yourself," I said while Wesley said, "No."

Tora closed her eyes and sighed. "I'm not trying to be stubborn. That would be stupid. However, there are three of us. Terrible odd number if I do say so myself. Someone needs to stay here in case the others make their way back. Cori, you know Mr. Hayes. Therefore, you need to go. Wesley, you have questions which I'm sure are important and need answering. Hence, leaving me here to hold down the fort while not thinking the worst about this whole situation."

I was wrong. She's smart and brave. "I hate the number three, too." It was the worst to have in a time like this. The thought of leaving anyone alone always makes me uneasy, but out here it's times ten.

Wesley's face twisted with worry, but he didn't argue again. He couldn't argue against the logic of what she said. "Be careful, okay?"

Tora took a deep breath and let it out dramatically. "I think my biggest enemy will be my mind, but I'll be careful of what I think."

With that settled, Wesley and I set off to get Mr. Hayes.

Chapter Eighteen

Amara

Ashten sobbed quietly in my arms. Her whole body was trembling with exhaustion and fear. I held her tightly and tried to be the steady presence she desperately needed, even though my own heart hammered painfully in my chest.

"It's okay," I whispered into her hair, smoothing it gently with one shaking hand. "You're safe now. We're here, and we're going to get out of this. I promise."

She clung to me harder, her voice muffled and broken. "I was lost. The forest... it kept shifting, like it was alive. Like it was trapping me. I didn't know where I was and felt like I was starting to lose myself."

I shivered, understanding exactly what she meant. "Trust me, I understand. But look, we found you. That's what matters now."

Behind me, Laken moved quietly through the rubble of the barn. He was still searching methodically for my mother's EMF meter. He was almost frantic. I knew he believed finding it could be our only chance at evading this nightmare and getting everyone out safely.

I tightened my hold on Ashten, rocking her gently. "Breathe," I said softly. "Just breathe. You're okay. We're going to be okay."

She drew in a ragged breath, but her tears still came quietly.

"Amara!" Laken called suddenly, urgency spiking in his voice.

My heart lurched as I turned toward him. "Did you find it?"

He hesitated, his expression unreadable. His eyes were locked onto something beneath the collapsed loft. "I found something. You need to see this."

I glanced down at Ashten. I was reluctant to let go of her even for a moment.

She wiped her eyes and nodded weakly. "Go," she whispered. "I'm okay."

I carefully released her, helping her lean against a sturdy beam, before quickly crossing the debris-strewn floor to Laken.

"What is it?" I asked, voice tight.

He pointed to something hidden beneath splintered boards and rotting hay. My breath caught in my throat as I knelt down beside him and brushed away the dirt. It was my mother's coat, folded and carefully hidden beneath some boards. Wrapped safely in its fabric was the EMF meter. From the looks of it, it was as if it had been placed there on purpose. My hand shook as I reached out and touched the worn fabric.

Laken's eyes met mine, dark with understanding. "Your mom was a smart woman. She probably knew you'd come out here looking for answers. She left this for you."

With shaking hands, I slowly pulled the EMF meter from within her coat. The familiar shape was heavy in my palm. "She knew something was going to happen to her," I whispered, hating that truth.

I carefully handed the EMF meter to Laken, but held onto my mother's coat. It still smelled like her. "Do you know how many nights I watched my mother hunched over her workbench, carefully tweaking the delicate sensors inside?" The memories are raw and painful. "She was obsessed with getting it right. Little did I know what she was doing."

"She was obsessed because she knew something was out here that needed to be stopped." He exhaled softly, almost reverently, as he studied the meter. "It still looks well intact."

I swallowed, pushing away the tightness in my throat as I nodded. "Good."

Laken urgently glanced around. "We should gather up everything else while we're here. Your sensors and the camera chip. Whatever data we have left could be critical."

I hesitated, glancing back at Ashten. She had pulled herself together somewhat, but she still looked fragile as she huddled against the barn beam. Laken gently touched my shoulder.

"I'll take care of her," he reassured me. "Get your equipment. We'll need every bit of evidence we can gather."

"Okay." I nodded firmly, believing him. If there was one thing I was sure about, it was Laken and his protection.

I went to the far side of the property where I knew some of the sensors were. My hands worked methodically as I carefully disconnected them and tucked each piece safely into my pack. As I did, I couldn't shake the feeling of being watched. I slowly turned in a circle and was relieved to find Laken watching across the expanse between us.

With the sensors safely secured, I moved quickly toward the edge of the clearing where my mother's camera had been placed. The housing was cracked, battered by weather and neglect. When I carefully pried it open, the chip inside was still intact.

I held it tightly between my fingers, a small surge of hope pulsing through me. Whatever truths lay hidden in this forest might be stored here.

"You good?" Laken's voice carried across the clearing, calm but anxious.

I tucked the chip securely into my pocket and stood to make my way back to him. "Yeah."

The afternoon sun was already slipping below the tangled tree line, casting long shadows across the ground. The forest around us seemed to darken rapidly.

"We should get going," I suggested.

Laken paused, glancing uneasily toward the sky. "We should wait until morning," he said, steady but cautious. "It's too risky to try and find camp in the dark."

I glanced toward Ashten, whose pale face looked drained beneath the dirt and tears. She nodded weakly. Exhaustion was etched into every line of her expression. "I don't want to go in the dark," she murmured. "Everything is worse at night."

I wanted to argue, but I also knew they were right. "Alright. Then we stay here until dawn."

We quickly cleared an area beneath the half-collapsed barn roof. Laken carefully tested the beams to ensure nothing would collapse on us in the night. The barn wasn't much, but it was shelter. It offered some barrier between us and the open woods.

Laken gathered dry wood and brush to build a small fire. I laid out the wool blanket and gently helped Ashten settle beside me. Her breathing was calmer now, though she still shivered occasionally. Her eyes would dart nervously toward every noise.

"Try to rest," I whispered, while squeezing her shoulder. "We'll get back safely tomorrow."

She gave me a weak nod, eyes fluttering closed as she leaned against my shoulder. Her breathing slowed almost immediately, exhaustion finally pulling her into sleep.

Laken settled on my other side, close enough that I could feel the comforting warmth of his body. He stared into the fire, brows furrowed. The EMF meter rested protectively in his lap. It was his comfort to head off what we couldn't see.

"Do you think they're alright back at camp?" I whispered after a moment, the worry finally slipping through my voice.

Laken sighed softly, his eyes gentle but uncertain. "They're tough. Wesley knows what he's doing."

I nodded slowly, biting my lip. "I hope you're right."

His hand found mine, fingers gently squeezing reassurance. "We'll find them in the morning."

I wanted to believe him. I needed to believe him. But as darkness fully descended around us, and the whispers of the forest rose once more, certainty was something I couldn't quite reach.

Hours passed, with neither one of us truly resting. Laken gathered dry branches and bits of broken timber to keep the fire burning. The flames felt comforting against the darkness, even if the sense of safety was an illusion.

Ashten stirred in her sleep and grumbled, "I'm hungry."

I opened my backpack. There wasn't much, a few granola bars, some trail mix, and a small pack of dried fruit, but I carefully divided it up.

"Here," I murmured gently, passing a portion to Ashten. She took it with shaking hands and offered me a weak thanks. I gave Laken his portion, which he took with gratitude. We were all tired, hungry, and stressed out.

Ashten curled up beside me when we finished eating, her eyes glistening with fresh tears. "I just want to go home," she whispered, her voice breaking as her composure finally crumbled.

"I know," I said softly, gently guiding her head into my lap. "We will. I promise. Just rest now."

Her tears came quietly at first, then deeper, more ragged, until her shoulders shook with each sob. I stroked her hair softly, holding her close as she cried herself into a restless sleep. My chest tightened painfully, guilt and worry twisting together.

Across the fire, Laken watched silently, his expression blank. After a moment, his eyes softened with reassurance. "We'll get her home," he whispered firmly. "We'll get everyone home."

I nodded, but couldn't find the words to respond. Ashten's breathing finally settled, her head heavy and warm in my lap.

"We can't ignore this anymore, Amara," Laken said, breaking the silence.

I glanced up at him, startled by his quiet intensity. "Ignore what?"

He ran a tired hand through his hair, the firelight flickering in his eyes. "What's happening out here. You've always wanted logical explanations, and I respect that. But whatever this is," he paused, searching my face. "It's beyond logic."

I shook my head, swallowing down the unease rising in my chest. "There's always an explanation, Laken. Always. It might be strange or complicated, but that doesn't mean it's not rational. We just have to find it."

He watched me carefully, his expression gentle but firm. "I know you want that. But sometimes, logic just doesn't apply." He hesitated for a heartbeat before adding, "Maybe your mom knew that, too."

I flinched, his words hitting closer to home than I wanted. My throat tightened. "Maybe. But that doesn't mean I'm going to stop trying."

He moved closer, the firelight softening his features. "We won't stop. But, I need you to understand something." His voice lowered, firm yet gentle. "I will do whatever it takes to get us out of here. I won't let anything happen to you. Ever."

Something in the sincerity of his words cracked the last bit of resistance in my heart. I reached over slowly, my fingers trembling as they found his hand. He squeezed gently, grounding me in a way nothing else had in days.

Without another word, Laken moved closer, scooting quietly so as not to disturb Ashten. His strong arms wrapped gently around me, pulling me against him. For a brief moment, my breath hitched. A wave of fear tightened in my chest, but then his warmth comforted me.

"I've got you," he murmured against my hair.

I leaned into him, eyes fluttering closed as the steady beat of his heart soothed something raw inside me. Whatever this was, whatever the forest wanted, at least I wasn't facing it alone.

Chapter Nineteen

Amara

I jolted awake, my heart racing in the darkness. For a long, terrifying moment, I had no idea where I was. Dark shapes loomed around me, distorted by shadows and weak moonlight filtering through cracks in the trees. My breath came in short, rapid bursts. Panic twisted in my chest like a vice.

Where was I?

I turned slowly, eyes wide, straining to see. "Laken?" My voice was small, barely audible. Darkness swallowed it. "Ashten?"

No response. Fear clawed at my throat, choking me.

How did I get here? I racked my brain, struggling to piece together the night. Everything was fuzzy.

My pulse thundered painfully, and I forced myself to breathe. Think. I had to think.

We were at the homestead, weren't we? We'd found something. Something important, but the details were slipping away and leaving me to grasp at empty air. Tears stung in my eyes as fear began to consume me.

"Laken!" I called louder, desperation creeping into my voice.

Silence answered me.

I pushed myself slowly to my feet, my legs weak and trembling. Where were the others? Had something happened to them?

A chilling thought hit me suddenly, piercing through the fog and fear.

What if the forest had finally claimed them?

Heart pounding, I stumbled forward, trying to navigate the darkness that pressed in from every direction. Without my flashlight, each step felt uncertain. Branches clawed at my face and arms as I blindly moved deeper into the woods, guided only by panic and desperation.

My sobs broke the silence. They were raw and ugly. Everywhere around me, the forest whispered. The trees creaked as the leaves rustled. A faint voice was intermingled with nature's music.

"Hello?" My voice trembled in the stillness, each syllable quivering with a mixture of hope and fear, but only the trees responded. Their leaves rustled like distant whispers in the oppressive silence.

I quickened my pace, my heart racing as I navigated the darkened path. My feet stumbled over hidden roots and jagged stones. The chill of the night air wrapped around me like a shroud, and my breath came in sharp gasps. Each inhale was laced with the bitter tang of adrenaline as my growing terror gnawed at my insides.

Then, without warning, the ground beneath me crumbled away, plunging me into an abyss of uncertainty.

I cried out sharply, tumbling forward, hands grasping uselessly at air as I plunged down the steep incline. Pain shot through my limbs as I rolled uncontrollably, branches and rocks battering my body.

I hit the bottom hard, my head striking something solid, sending a sharp jolt of agony through my skull. My vision exploded with bright stars, then darkness swept in swiftly, swallowing me whole.

Chapter Twenty

Wesley

Amara was definitely going to kill us for this, but there was no other option. Cori stood silently at my side, shifting anxiously as we waited on the front porch of Mr. Hayes's house. The porch light illuminated our every move. Each second felt like an eternity.

The door finally swung open, revealing Mr. Haye's stern face, etched with confusion and concern.

"Wesley? Cori?" His brow furrowed as his gaze traveled over us. I will say we didn't look the best, what with our ragged, blood-stained clothes. I could only imagine what our distressed faces looked like. "What's going on? Where's Amara?"

I swallowed hard, glancing nervously at Cori before meeting his eyes again. "She's lost in the forest and we need your help."

He didn't move, but his jaw tightened sharply. "I told her that damn project was dangerous. What happened?"

I steadied myself, pushing past the ache in my injured leg and the shame rising in my throat. "We all got separated. Laken and Amara went looking for Ashten and Cori. Cori made it back on her own, but Laken, Ashten, and Amara are still missing."

His expression darkened as worry replaced his anger. He stepped back, gesturing us inside. "Come in. Tell me everything."

As we stepped inside, Cori softly closed the door behind us. The walls were alive with photographs of Amara, each telling a piece of her story. One picture, however, truly captivated me. In it, Amara was smiling joyfully alongside a woman I could only guess was her mother. They were sharing a moment that seemed precious, both radiating happiness. Amara looked to be in her teens, and from everything I knew about her, I couldn't help but think that such moments of joy were likely few and far between.

We sat in the living room, and I recounted every detail I could remember: the sensors we placed, the strange readings, the unsettling occurrences, the screams in the forest, and the terrifying way Tora had been lifted into the air. I explained how I'd gotten injured, separated from Tora, and how Amara and Laken had set off into the woods searching for Cori and Ashten.

"And Cori?" Mr. Hayes asked, turning toward her. His voice softened slightly, noticing her obvious exhaustion. "You made it back alone?"

She nodded weakly, her eyes shadowed. "Barely. I don't know how to describe it other than the forest kept changing. I became disoriented a lot. Thankfully, I smelled the campfire and found my way back."

Mr. Hayes leaned forward, rubbing his temples. His face was drawn with worry. "I warned Amara not to go into those damn woods. I told her it wasn't a place to meddle with, but she promised to be safe."

"We know," I said quietly. "And she was until we all got separated."

He stood slowly as a deep determination settled in his eyes. "Let's go get my daughter."

I hesitated for a moment as he grabbed his coat. My unanswered questions lodged in my throat. I needed some information before we left, but it meant bringing up painful memories. Suddenly, I didn't want to ask them.

Cori stood silently by my side, watching him with anxious eyes. She nudged me forward and mouthed *hurry.* She was right. I was losing my chance.

"Mr. Hayes," I finally said. "Did Esme ever tell you about her research? About what she really thought was happening out there?" My palms began to sweat, and my glasses fogged at the edges. I wasn't sure how he would react to the question.

His movements paused, and I caught the briefest flicker of hesitation cross his face before he shook his head sharply. "No. She kept most of it to herself. She knew I didn't like it."

I wasn't satisfied. The way he paused made me think there was something, but he wasn't sure of it either. "Are you sure?" I pressed gently. "Because last night, I had a dream. Well, a nightmare, really. But it felt real. In it, there was a woman. Her name was Malva Thaine."

Mr. Hayes froze, and his shoulders tensed noticeably. "Malva Thaine," he repeated softly, his voice tight with caution. "Where did you hear that name?"

"In the dream," I said quietly. "And Esme's journal."

Mr. Hayes slowly turned to face me, his expression guarded but undeniably shaken. "Esme, she mentioned Malva once or twice. She believed Malva's story was more than just folklore. I thought she was obsessed, losing herself in superstition. I refused to listen." He looked away, shame clouding his eyes. "Maybe that was my mistake."

I was sure to keep my tone respectful. I felt like I was intruding on something personal that was none of my business. "Did Esme ever say anything specifically about a curse? Anything at all?"

He shook his head immediately, but then paused. His expression shifted as a distant memory surfaced. "There was one night," he began slowly, voice low and strained, "she woke up frantic. She kept rambling about blood ties and how they bound her to that place. I thought it was just a nightmare, nonsense from spending too much time in those woods."

"What exactly did she say?" I pressed gently.

Mr. Hayes's gaze met mine, a shadow passing through his expression. "She said, 'It started with two, and ends with two.' She kept repeating it, over and over. I didn't understand it, but I remember the fear in her voice."

My pulse quickened. "Two," I repeated softly, glancing briefly at Cori. Mr. Hayes's words lingered in the air like the last echo of a warning.

It started with two, and ends with two.

I stared at him, heart thudding. The pieces were rearranging themselves in my mind. Two. Not just people. Not just a number, but bloodlines.

It hit me like a jolt, and I turned to Cori. "We knew this probably had something to do with descendants of the town. They were the ones Malva targeted."

Mr. Hayes's brow furrowed, and he gave me a skeptical glance. "What are you getting at?"

"Answer me this," I said, trying to slow my racing thoughts. "All the people who've gone missing over the years, were they all locals? Born and raised in Greenwood or the surrounding area?"

His frown deepened, but after a beat, he nodded. "Yes, as far as I know, they were. Why?"

"Because Malva didn't just curse the land," I said quietly. "She cursed the town's bloodline. Any descendant of the townspeople who took her daughter from her. And if the forest recognizes that connection, it takes them. That could also be why outsiders never disappear. They just forget."

Mr. Reed stared at me for a long moment. "You think Amara's a descendant?"

"I know she is. Esme must've figured it out, too. That's why she was so obsessed. Why she kept going back. She was trying to stop it before it got her and Amara."

Mr. Hayes' brow pinched. "But you said two. Who is the other?"

"A descendant of Malva's," I said. "It started with two. It has to end with two. Malva cursed the land with her blood and the town's blood. Amara is the town's blood. If we can find Malva's descendant…"

"We might be able to stop it," he finished.

The air buzzed with purpose. We were close. Closer than anyone had ever been. Now, we just had to find the missing name.

I paused again, my mind racing as another question pressed urgently forward. "Mr. Hayes, did Esme ever find a living descendant of Malva's? Someone who could help make sense of all this?"

He shook his head. "I know she tried, though I didn't know why. She spent months looking through local histories, genealogies, and everything else she could find."

"How can there be no one?" Cori asked softly, disappointment evident in her voice.

"I don't know," he said quietly. "But if there were any descendants, Esme never discovered them. She searched and even traveled to neighboring towns, but every trail ended in a dead end. Eventually, she stopped looking."

Mr. Hayes abruptly turned for the door. "We're wasting time. I should've gone after Amara the second you walked through my door."

I stepped toward him, slowly, not to challenge him but to steady the moment. "I get it," I said, meeting his gaze. "She's your daughter. I'd do the same if it were me."

His eyes narrowed slightly. He knew a but was coming, and it was.

"But listen," I continued, voice even. "Going after her now, without understanding what we're walking into, won't help. Esme knew the curse started with two. If we're right, we need to find a descendant of Malva's. That's the key. Not just to save Amara, but to stop the curse for good."

He stared at me, frustration etched into every line of his face.

"I'm not asking you to sit on your hands," I added quickly. "I'm asking you to help me do the only thing that might actually work. I know Amara. She's going to fight. We have to fight right back with her."

A long beat passed. Then he exhaled, shoulders falling just slightly as the fire in his expression turned from panic to focus. "There's one place that might have the records we need," he said. "The genealogy department at the Cedarbrook City Hall. Esme tried getting access to them several times but was always denied. If there's a surviving branch of Malva's line, it'll be in there."

"We'll have to wait until tomorrow to get permission," Cori said, frustration lacing her words.

Mr. Hayes walked over to a table by the door. He picked up the toolbox sitting on top. A dark look glinted in his eyes. "I don't need anyone's permission."

Chapter Twenty-One

Amara

My eyes fluttered open. The world blurred and spun around me. Pain radiated from the back of my skull, pulsing sharply as I struggled to sit up. Everything felt out of focus.

Where was I?

I forced myself upright, my body swaying unsteadily as I blinked into the surrounding darkness. I shivered uncontrollably, the night air pressed cold and heavy against my skin.

"Laken?" My voice barely escaped as a whisper. "Ashten?"

Only silence answered me, a thick, suffocating quiet.

Slowly, I stood. Every muscle ached with protest. The forest felt unsettling, like it was watching. I stumbled forward, unsure which direction I'd even come from. The dizziness continued to make my head spin. Every tree looked the same, every path identical, with no familiar landmarks.

"Hello?" I called louder, desperation creeping into my voice. My pulse quickened with fear. "Is anyone there?"

The wind whispered back, soft and mocking.

It's not real, I tried reassuring myself. *It can't be real.*

As the darkness pressed closer, the certainty I'd always clung to was slipping away. Every step felt heavier than the last. Branches clawed at my skin, scraping against my arms and legs, leaving trails of stinging pain behind. My breathing grew labored, my heartbeat echoing loudly in my ears.

Words of defeat crept insidiously into my mind, whispering in a voice that felt achingly familiar but not my own.

Give up.

I stumbled forward, flinching as another branch tore painfully across my cheek.

You can't win.

The pain grew sharper, burning across my skin, and my muscles screamed for relief. It felt like the forest was determined to break me, wearing me down one painful wound at a time.

You're not strong enough.

I shook my head desperately, eyes stinging with tears. "No," I whispered hoarsely. "I can't stop. I won't."

The forest pressed in tighter, and the whispers were louder now, more insistent.

You're already lost. Just like your mother.

I stopped abruptly, panic surging through me, heart seizing in my chest. A deep, shuddering sob tore from my throat. "No," I whispered again, voice shaking. "Please, stop."

I forced myself forward once more, knowing that every step might lead me further into oblivion. Still, I wouldn't stop. I had to keep moving.

Then, an urgent and achingly familiar voice came through the dark veil of despair and pain.

"Amara!"

I froze, breath catching in my throat. I wasn't sure if the voice was real or another cruel trick played by the forest.

"Amara! Where are you?" The voice was louder now, edged with desperation and raw with emotion.

Footsteps grew louder, crunching through the underbrush as they drew nearer. Panic rose in my throat, and I instinctively stumbled back as a figure materialized from the shadows. My heart raced fiercely, pounding like a drum in my chest, a primal fear coursing through me. How did this person know my name?

He reached me in an instant, his strong hands gripping my shoulders gently yet firmly. "Amara. Oh, thank God."

I stared up at him, my vision blurred. Confusion was still clouding my mind. Who was this? He felt familiar, but my mind resisted recognition.

"Who are you?" My voice cracked, barely a whisper.

His touch was gentle as he cupped my face between his palms and brushed away the tears with his thumbs. "It's me," he said softly. "It's Laken."

My vision sharpened, his face slowly coming into focus beneath the dim glow of moonlight. Those grey eyes, piercing and steady, searched mine desperately. Suddenly, memories flooded back like a breaking wave, vivid and powerful.

The first time we kissed beneath the summer stars.

The nights we'd spent laughing until dawn.

The softness of his gaze as we made love, his eyes locked onto mine, anchoring me, holding me close even when the world around us threatened to unravel.

"Laken," I whispered, my voice trembling with relief and longing.

He exhaled deeply, pulling me into his arms. He held me tightly as though afraid to ever let go. I clung to him fiercely, basking in his familiar warmth. His heartbeat was steady and strong against mine.

"You found me," I choked out, my voice breaking.

"I'll always find you," he murmured fiercely, pressing his lips gently against my forehead. "Always."

I pulled back just enough to look at him, my fingers still clutching the front of his jacket. "How did you find me?" I whispered, my voice trembling.

He brushed his thumb across my cheek. "I woke up and you were gone. I didn't care how dark it was or where the forest tried to lead me. I just kept going. I followed every instinct I had."

My chest tightened, and tears welled up in my eyes again. It wasn't from fear this time, but from the overwhelming relief of hearing those words and truly feeling his presence. He stood right in front of me when I thought I had been swallowed by something I couldn't escape.

"You shouldn't have," I murmured, shaking my head. Guilt rose in my throat. "It's too dangerous out here."

"So is losing you," he said without missing a beat. "I wasn't about to let that happen."

We stood there clinging to one another. The lingering weight of fear slowly began to lift. My head still throbbed, and my thoughts came in pieces, but I was beginning to feel like myself again. Laken's presence helped anchor me.

I turned my head toward him, my voice soft. "Where's Ashten?"

He gazed at the trees, a subtle crease defining his forehead. "When I told her you were gone, she panicked. I managed to calm her down and promised that I would find you. I even handed her my compass and told her to wait until sunrise before following it west. It'll lead her straight back to camp. She should be fine."

"Should be?" I echoed, my voice wavering. A familiar dread began to creep into my chest once more.

"She listens when it counts. She'll make it," Laken assured me.

I took a moment to absorb his words, allowing that flicker of hope to nestle within me. Ashten's fire might have waned, but it was far from extinguished. She was a fighter.

"How are we supposed to find our way out?" My chin trembled as uncertainty flooded my thoughts. "The forest keeps changing."

Laken brushed his thumb gently along my cheek, his gaze unwavering. "Then we find a way to make it out. We can't give up now."

Caught off guard by the steady resolve in his voice, I blinked at him.

He offered a small, crooked smile. "We'll figure it out. We always do."

Chapter Twenty-Two

Wesley

The room had grown heavy with silence, save for the occasional creak of the old wooden floor and the soft rustle of papers beneath our fingers. Mr. Hayes paced near the window like a caged animal, his jaw clenched tight. His eyes would dart between the tree line beyond the glass and the table covered in old records and printouts. His agitation was mounting by the minute. I didn't blame him. Amara was still out there.

"We're wasting time," he muttered, his voice low and sharp. "My daughter could be in danger. Every second we sit here flipping through the past, she's further away."

Cori looked up from where she sat across from me, her expression strained but steady. "Mr. Hayes, we all agreed that rushing in wildly would do us no good."

"She's right," I added, trying to keep my tone calm. "We're not doing nothing. If Esme was right, knowing who Malva's descendants were could change everything."

He let out a frustrated sigh and dragged a hand through his hair before planting his palms on the table's edge. "I should've gone after her the second you walked through my door."

"And ended up lost too?" Cori countered gently, standing now, her voice firm. "She could be anywhere in that forest, and you know what it does to people who go in blind. If you go now, angry and desperate, the forest will consume you."

Mr. Hayes didn't respond immediately. He just stared at the mess of records and maps.

"I get it," I said quietly. "She's your daughter. But this curse is bigger than any of us. We can't fight it without understanding it. We're close, I can feel it."

He finally looked back at us, and something in his eyes shifted. Determination. "One more hour," he said. "Then I'm going in, whether you've found something or not."

Fair enough.

I turned another dusty page, the musty scent of ancient paper filling my lungs as I squinted at the faded ink. I struggled to make sense of the words as fatigue set in. A dull ache throbbed behind my eyes from the effort, yet an insistent nagging sensation stirred inside me, urging me to dig deeper. I began to notice that some of the dates didn't align correctly, creating a dissonance in the chronology.

With a flick of my wrist, I flipped back and forth through the fragile pages, desperately trying to connect the scattered dots. Each turn brought a mix of hope and frustration. It was like a crucial piece of a puzzle was eluding my grasp.

My thoughts clicked into place as I realized there was a significant gap in the records. "Look at this," I muttered, sitting up straighter. "There's a section missing from the town records here. Between 1963 and 1966, there's nothing on the Thaine family. There's nothing on any family."

Cori leaned over the table beside me, brow furrowed. "That doesn't make sense. Did they relocate? Change their name?"

I scanned further back, heart pounding a little faster. I traced the family tree back to start again. "Malva had a younger sister named Lettie Thaine. There's no mention of her in Esme's journal."

Mr. Hayes immediately turned back from the window, eyes narrowing. "What happened to her?"

"She stayed in Cedarbrook, looks like," I said, flipping another page. "The last trace I see of the family is a Clara Sutton, born 1939."

"I know that name," Cori said suddenly. "Hang on." She moved to the laptop we had set up and typed rapidly. A moment later, her face went pale. "Wes, I think I found her." She turned the screen toward me. It was a scanned newspaper clipping from 1965. The headline hit me like a punch to the chest:

"Tragic Collision on County Route 7: Expectant Mother and Husband Killed in Freak Accident"

I leaned in, my eyes darting across the page. Excitement bubbled within me, and my palms grew clammy as my heart raced with every word I read.

"Clara Sutton, 26, and her husband were returning from a prenatal appointment when their car lost control and collided with a logging truck. Both were pronounced dead at the scene." I paused for a minute before continuing. "Doctors at Cedarbrook General were able to perform an emergency cesarean. The infant survived and is in stable condition."

"Oh my god," Cori whispered. "The baby survived."

"There's no name listed," Mr. Hayes said, his eyes scanning the article as he leaned over us. "Just 'baby girl.'"

"Are there any adoption records?"

I flipped through the town records while Cori searched the internet. I shook my head, frustrated. "Nothing yet. It just ends."

The trail ended abruptly after the accident with no further records of the baby girl who'd survived. No birth certificate, no official adoption paperwork. But something wasn't sitting right. The town was small, the kind of place where secrets were often quietly buried under familiar names.

I returned to the adoption records, which were not available in digital format but carefully preserved in a collection of photocopied archives. The dimly lit room was filled with tall shelves, stacked with thick binders that contained countless personal stories. I sifted through each file meticulously, focusing on those dating from late 1965 to early 1966, determined to uncover any information that might lead me closer to my goal.

The task was labor-intensive, requiring nearly an hour of cross-referencing names, dates, and other details. Mr. Hayes paced quietly behind me, his soft footsteps reminding me of the deadline. However, it seemed he was allowing that deadline to slip away since we were onto something important. Papers rustled softly as I turned them over. Then, amidst the yellowing pages, I found her name. Sarah Wilkenson.

The file indicated that her adoption was finalized in January 1966. However, the information was sparse. No parents were listed; it was just a solitary note stating the adoption had been processed through a private family attorney. This lack of detail intrigued and frustrated me, igniting a mystery about Sarah's early life and the circumstances surrounding her adoption.

"This has to be her," I whispered, my pulse spiking. "It lines up exactly with the timeline. She would've been born right after the accident. Private adoption, no paper trail, but she stayed in Cedarbrook."

Mr. Hayes stepped closer, the name clearly resonating with him. "Sarah Wilkenson." He rubbed his chin, eyes narrowing. "I know her, although it's now Wilkenson anymore. It's McCure. She still lives in town. Keeps to herself mostly. She works out at the old ranger station on the east end. I didn't know—" He paused. "Esme never made the connection."

"No one did," I said.

Mr. Hayes looked at me, his face drawn but resolute. "You think this'll work? That involving her could stop it?"

"I don't know," I admitted. We wouldn't know for sure until we tested our theory. It was far from the experiment we'd initially set out to make when we left the university. "But it's our only shot."

Cori grabbed her coat without a word, already moving toward the door.

Mr. Hayes nodded once. "Let's go."

As we left City Hall, Mr. Hayes propped a brick against the door to keep it shut. The busted door lock lay useless on the ground. The clock tower chimed, and I glanced up to see it was nearing midnight. It had already been dark for too long.

"We need to hurry," I said, my frantic tone urging everyone along.

Chapter Twenty-Three

Amara

As the first hints of light crept into the sky, I struggled to shake off the remnants of the night. My throbbing headache pulsed in rhythm with my heartbeat. My joints were stiff, and my throat felt like sandpaper. Gathering my thoughts felt like trying to catch smoke with my bare hands, elusive and frustrating.

What day is it?

How long have I been out here?

Why can't I remember... anything?

I pushed myself upright with trembling arms, each movement slow and disconnected, like I wasn't entirely inside my own body. My thoughts were murky. Faces blurred. Names slipped through my fingers like water.

That's when I saw him.

A figure, lying motionless beside me. His back was to me, one arm curled awkwardly beneath him. Panic prickled at the edges of my fog. I crawled toward him, my breath shallow, heart thumping. I reached out, hesitating for a moment before gently rolling him onto his back.

He was young. His clothes were torn and smudged with dirt. His dark hair was damp and stuck to his forehead, and his face... Something about the line of his jaw, the curve of his lips, and the faint scar beneath his brow meant something. Did I know him?

My heart told me I knew him. My mind refused to agree.

"Hey," I whispered, voice cracking as I lightly touched his shoulder. "Can you hear me?"

His eyes fluttered open and squinted against the morning light. When he looked at me, something in me twisted, tight and urgent.

"Amara," he rasped.

The name struck me like a bell. It was familiar but odd. Was it my name? I didn't know. Panic clawed its way through me, igniting a fierce rush of adrenaline that made me feel lightheaded.

When the boy reached out for my hand, I instinctively jerked back. I scrambled away from him on hands and heels, my breath catching.

"Don't!" I choked out, my voice raw and unfamiliar in my ears. "Don't come near me."

His face twisted with pain. "Amara, it's me. It's Laken."

The name echoed again in my mind, hollow and distant. Laken. *Laken.* I should know him, but I didn't. I didn't even know myself. My heart pulled toward him like a magnet, but my mind recoiled, unable to bridge the gap. I couldn't remember his touch, his voice, his smile. There was only a deep ache that told me I'd lost something precious.

I looked around wildly, panic flaring in my chest. Trees surrounded us, towering and close. There was nowhere to run.

Then the wind began to howl. Suddenly and furiously, it came out of nowhere, slicing through the trees like a living thing. Branches creaked and groaned, leaves scattering in all directions as if something had been awakened.

The forest, once eerily still, began to move. The trees seemed to lean closer. The earth vibrated beneath my hands. Shadows stretched unnaturally long, and from the depths of the woods came a sound that raised every hair on my body. It was a low, distant whisper that mingled to sound like a thousand voices murmuring simultaneously.

The forest pulsed an unsettling energy that thrummed beneath the surface. It wasn't a welcoming sensation. Instead, it felt like the woods themselves were seething with a dark, uncontainable anger.

I pivoted back toward Laken. He was already clambering to his feet, his body swaying precariously as he reached out a trembling hand toward me. "We have to go," he insisted, urgency lacing his voice like a taut string ready to snap. "Now."

But my legs felt rooted to the spot. Panic simmered beneath my skin. I was paralyzed by uncertainty. Where would I even run to? And the gnawing doubt persisted. Could I trust him?

Suddenly, the stillness of the forest was shattered by a new sound. It was barely perceptible at first but grew more distinct—a jumble of scattered phrases and the muted thud of footsteps crunching through the tangled underbrush.

Fear coiled tightly in my chest, my heart stuttering erratically as the wind howled with an increasing ferocity. It was as if the forest was responding to their approach, rising up in rebellion against the intrusion. The trees creaked ominously, twisting in the wind, their branches clawing at the sky. Whispers surged through the air, frantic and agitated, as if something vital was unraveling around us.

The clearing shuddered beneath my feet. Figures emerged from the trees one by one, breathless and wide-eyed.

I was paralyzed, caught between instinct and a flicker of hope. Like a caught wild animal, I turned to run.

"Amara, sweetheart!" His voice resonated with authority, slicing through the fear that gripped me. With my heart racing, I turned back. The older man stood there, a protective barrier between me and the unknown faces behind him. His features held a haunting familiarity, but it was the warmth in his gaze that anchored me.

That look—deep, raw, and protective—reminded me of Laken's earlier today, but this was amplified. "You promised me you'd be safe," he reiterated, his voice softer now, tinged with worry.

My mind raced, scrambling to understand the past that connected us. Who was he? Why did he care so much? The world outside faded away as I searched his eyes, desperately seeking answers amid the chaos surrounding us.

Tears welled in his eyes. "Your mother used to make the same promise."

I sprang to my feet before my mind had a chance to catch up, my legs propelling me forward purely on instinct. A rush of relief swept over me. I enveloped him in a tight embrace, as if I were afraid to let go. "I'm sorry, Dad," I murmured into the fabric of his shirt, the words barely escaping my lips as emotion tightened my throat.

Blinking to see past the tears, the others came into focus. My family. They all hugged one another as they watched the exchange. But there was someone else, someone I honestly didn't recognize. Her dark hair was pulled into a braid, and her eyes scanned the trees like she could hear things we couldn't.

My dad pulled back to look at me. "It's okay," he said softly. "You're okay now."

I scanned the faces around me, taking in my friends who had gathered with worried expressions, my father standing resolutely at the edge of the group, and the enigmatic stranger whose presence was both unsettling and intriguing. Clarity began to break through the haze that had clouded my thoughts. The warmth of Laken's hand pressed firmly against my back provided a reassuring anchor, grounding me amidst the swirling confusion. I could feel the gentle strength of their support as I took a deep breath, feeling the fog of uncertainty begin to lift.

Seeing this shift in me, Wesley stepped forward. "I kept my promise," he began, his voice steady and eager. "I figured out what your mom was onto. It was a curse—a darkness that stretches far beyond our understanding. Esme discovered that it all started with Malva Thaine, a woman consumed by vengeance for her daughter's life. In her wrath, she cursed not only the town's descendants but her own bloodline as well. To end this cycle, it requires two. Two descendants."

He shifted his gaze between me and the girl beside him. "This is Sarah. She carries the blood of Malva. And you are a descendant of the town itself."

Confusion swirled in my mind. "What does that mean?" I asked, panic creeping into my voice. "I don't understand."

Wesley took a breath, his expression growing somber. "Your mother left behind a trail of notes, sketches, fragments of the truth buried in her research. In a dream, I glimpsed what she encountered. *'Those who trespass will lose their way and wander until the forest claims them. And if their blood bleeds true, may they find their damnation.'*"

His words reverberated within me, igniting an unease that prickled at the edges of my consciousness. The forest around us was still, as if it had paused in silent anticipation.

But then Wesley's voice softened, cutting through the dread. "But perhaps if the blood bleeds true together, it doesn't damn you. It frees you."

A glimmer of hope flickered in the pervasive darkness, igniting a spark within me that urged me to believe our intertwined destinies could lead to salvation rather than an inevitable ruin. I turned to Sarah, who stood immobile a few steps behind my father. Her body was tense and still as if she were encased in stone. Her expression was an impenetrable mask.

"Sarah?" I called softly, my voice cutting through the oppressive silence that hung in the air.

Her wide, terrified eyes locked onto mine, and I could see the fear clinging to her. "I don't know if I can do this," she murmured, her voice barely above a whisper. "I didn't ask for this. I don't even know what it means." The quiver in her tone spoke volumes of the turmoil raging inside her.

I took a cautious step closer, my heart aching at the sight of her vulnerability. "You're not alone," I reassured her, reaching out as if to bridge the distance between us. "None of us asked for this. But the forest chose us, whether we understand it or not. Right now, you might be the only one who can help me survive it."

Her gaze fell to the ground, her jaw quivering ever so slightly as she pressed her hand against her chest, as if trying to steady the frantic pounding of her heart. The weight of her confession hung in the air. "I've felt it my whole life," she continued, her voice a fragile thread. "Like something's been pulling at me from the shadows. And now I find out I'm part of this?" She glanced toward the deep woods. "All those people who died... It was my family's fault."

Wesley stepped forward, his voice gentle yet firm, cutting through Sarah's self-doubt. "You're more than just a part of this," he said, his eyes steady on her. "You might be what ends it."

Sarah closed her eyes, letting out a shaky breath as she tried to collect herself. For a moment, she was lost in thought. Fear was still present in her features, but a spark of determination began to break through the shadows. When she finally opened her eyes again, I could see a mix of fear and resolve reflected in her gaze.

"Okay," she whispered, her voice steadier now, filled with newfound strength. "Let's end it."

With a deep breath, Sarah took a step toward me, her hand trembling as she drew a small knife from her pocket. The blade glinted in the faint light, and I saw the hesitation lingering in her eyes, the internal conflict evident in the way her fingers shook. Yet, with a flicker of courage, she offered the blade to me.

I nodded and gently took it from her, my own hands shaking. Sarah winced slightly as I pressed the blade into her palm. Then I cut my own. Blood welled to the surface, warm and red.

We turned to confront the vast expanse of the forest, its trees looming over the land. Our hands instinctively reached for one another, fingers intertwining as if guided by a force beyond ourselves. As our palms pressed together, tiny droplets of bright red blood mingled, forming glossy crimson jewels that fell onto the rich, dark soil beneath us. The world fell into a profound stillness.

Chapter Twenty-Four

Amara

The moment our blood hit the earth of the forest floor, an uncanny transformation enveloped the air around us.

It began subtly, with a singular breath drawn from the towering trees, as if they had collectively exhaled in synchrony. A brisk, biting wind surged through the clearing, swirling around us in a languid spiral. It didn't rustle the leaves or sway the branches. Instead, it beckoned, urging the very essence of the woods toward us. The ground beneath our feet rumbled softly, a deep, resonant vibration reverberating through our bones.

Sarah's grip on my hand tightened, the warmth of her blood mingling with my own. We stood transfixed, unyielding, as the forest around us burst into a vibrant existence. It was vibrant yet foreboding.

The trees groaned low and mournfully, their bark splitting open in places and their branches twisting inward, drawn toward the sacred circle we had unwittingly forged. Shadows thickened at our feet, pooling like dark liquid, while the light filtering from above seemed to dim. It was as though the sun had been ensnared behind a thick, ominous veil.

From behind me, Wesley inhaled sharply, the sound slicing through the thick tension, while Cori whispered a quiet prayer, her words barely audible amidst the mounting energy. Even my father moved closer, his protective instincts igniting like a flame.

And then, the voices emerged. Not just one, but many.

They whispered from the trees and the very soil cradling us. A thousand murmurs collided, some steeped in sorrow, others laced with anger, while a few bore an aching longing that filled my eyes with tears unbidden.

Suddenly, Sarah's knees buckled, and I swiftly caught her, steadying her trembling form. Her face had drained of color, and her wide, haunted eyes reflected a sight only she could perceive.

"I see them," she murmured, her voice barely more than a breath. "They're all around us."

Then the wind abruptly stopped. The vibrant forest around us fell into an unparalleled silence, the kind that made every breath feel loud in comparison.

In that stillness, a sound emerged, soft yet distinct. It echoed the rhythm of a heartbeat. *One. Two*. Each pulse seemed to resonate with the foundation of the Earth.

Suddenly, the ground beneath us split. A crack formed in the soil, precisely where our blood had fell. From that sacred union, two delicate shoots of green emerged. They unfurled rapidly, stretching toward the heavens like eager vines yearning for the sun's embrace.

Life! It sprang forth from the very spot where death had held dominion for far too long.

The curse that had bound us was rewriting itself. It was unwinding, loosening its grip on our fates.

An unseen force seemed to flow through me, a wave of sensations that was both cold and warm at once. The heavy burden I'd been bearing lifted. I gasped in astonishment, my hands instinctively clutching Sarah, who, beside me, released a heartfelt sob.

It was over. The tension that had knotted our lives together with despair had unraveled.

The forest had accepted our offering, embracing it as part of its eternal cycle. In return, it had set us free.

Chapter Twenty-Five

Amara

We finally broke through the thick curtain of trees, stepping into the clearing that had become our makeshift home. Our camp lay before us, patiently waiting for our return.

Ashten was the first to spot us. She rose slowly from her crouch beside the crackling fire, blinking in disbelief. Her mouth formed a silent gasp, and her hand instinctively flew to her chest as if to hold back the swell of emotions.

"Amara!"

Before I could prepare myself, she charged at me. The impact knocked the breath from my lungs. Her arms wrapped tightly around my neck, her embrace surprisingly strong. Tears streamed down her cheeks, dampening my shoulder as she pressed her face into me. She clung to me as if I were a lifeline she feared losing again. "I thought you were dead," she sobbed, her voice thick with emotion. "I swore you were dead."

In response, I held her just as fiercely, allowing her tears to soak into my clothing. I welcomed the familiar scent of her coconut shampoo. The oppressive weight of the forest began to peel away from me like the heavy, wet leaves of fall.

Eventually, she pulled back, and her eyes were now red from crying yet glimmering with an unmistakable spark of hope and joy. "Don't ever do that again, you dumb bitch," she said, voice cracking, but there it was. That spark. That familiar flame.

"I missed your tender affection," I smiled, voice rough but steady.

"You should. You don't get hugs like that twice."

Laughter rippled through the camp.

And in that moment, surrounded by people who'd fought to bring me back, and those who never stopped believing I could return, I finally knew... This is what family was all about.

Later, after the emotions had settled, I found Wesley sitting off to the side with a notebook in his lap. He was scribbling furiously, probably trying to capture every detail before it slipped away.

I approached quietly and sank down beside him.

He didn't look up. "You alive for real this time, or am I hallucinating?"

I smiled faintly. "Very real. I checked."

He finally glanced over at me, and despite the apparent exhaustion lining his face, there was a spark of relief behind his glasses.

I nudged his arm gently. "Thank you. For everything. For not giving up on me."

Wesley chuckled, shutting the notebook. "Yeah, well... I always said I wanted to be the guy who finally debunked ghosts. You know, put the spooky myths to bed with some science and logic."

"And?" I asked, raising an eyebrow.

He grinned crookedly. "Let's just say, maybe there's something logic to Black people being scared of spirits. Don't mess with them because they will mess with you back."

I laughed, the sound catching me off guard after everything. It felt good.

"But I couldn't have done it without you," I said, still smiling. "We all couldn't."

Wesley shrugged like it was no big deal, but the proud glint in his eyes said otherwise. "Next time you run off to prove a theory in a cursed forest, take a sage stick."

"Deal."

The sun hung low on the horizon, bathing the campsite in a warm, golden hue that danced through the leaves of the surrounding trees. The enticing aroma of something simmering over the fire wafted through the air, drawing us like moths to a flame toward the center of camp. Tora was there, her sleeves rolled up to her elbows, as she stood over the fire pit. She stirred a large pot, the contents bubbling and swirling, as if it held the key to comfort and normalcy amid the chaos of the past few days.

One by one, we drifted in, pulled by that savory, earthy scent, probably crafted from the last remnants of our dwindling supplies. There was something homey about the smell. It was like a warm embrace after a long, cold day.

"You shouldn't have," Cori said softly as she settled down beside Tora, her voice barely above a whisper, tinged with gratitude and exhaustion.

Tora shrugged but maintained her steady demeanor, even as fatigue creased her brow. "I didn't know what else to do while I waited. I had to do something," she replied, her voice resolute yet weary, echoing the unspoken sentiments of all of us.

No one dared to contradict her.

We gathered in a loose circle around the fire, holding bowls in our hands, with steam rising in gentle spirals into the cooling night air. Everyone ate in silence, the delicious warmth of the food almost too much to bear—too hungry, too anxious, and yet overwhelmingly grateful for this moment of stillness, this fragment of normalcy.

Sarah was the one to break it; her voice cut through the tranquility, tight with emotion. "Is it over?"

The air thickened with tension as everyone froze, the crackling of the fire suddenly the only sound to fill the void. Eyes darted around the circle—Cori, Wesley, Tora, my dad, Laken. Even Ashten, who typically lightened the mood with a well-timed quip, was uncharacteristically still.

Sarah's gaze fell upon me, searching for answers I wasn't sure I could provide.

I took a deep breath, feeling the warmth of the fire against my skin, and turned my gaze downward, letting it settle into the flickering flames.

"I don't know," I said truthfully. "I don't think any of us can be sure." My voice was soft but carried through the silence like a ripple. "The forest changed something. Maybe it was the curse. Maybe it was us. But the only thing we can be sure of..." I paused, looking around at the tired, bruised, and beautiful faces surrounding me. "Is that something unexplainable happened. Something real."

Heads nodded slowly. No one argued. They couldn't

As the fire settled into glowing embers and quiet conversations faded, I reached into my pack and pulled out two small, dirt-smudged items. The camera chip and one of the sensors I hadn't lost in the forest. They caught the firelight, dull and scratched, but still intact. I turned them over in my hands, feeling the weight of what they represented—everything we'd gone through, everything we still didn't understand.

"This doesn't mean we're done," I said, gazing at the group. "It doesn't mean we're going to stop trying to figure it out."

Wesley grinned, already leaning closer, eager to see what data survived.

Laken gave me a quiet nod, pride in his eyes.

And then—perfectly timed, just as I knew she would—Ashten groaned dramatically and flopped back onto her blanket.

"*Dios mío*," she muttered, dragging a hand over her face. "Here we go again."

Everyone laughed, even her.

Even me.

And beneath the stars and the scarred branches of Oak Hollow, something felt just a little bit lighter.

Not over.

But different.

And maybe... that was enough.

For now.

one year later...

I set the last box down with a soft thud and exhaled, brushing hair from my face as I looked around Laken's apartment, or rather, *our* apartment now.

It was small and chaotic but full of warm light and quiet promise. A record player sat in the corner with a stack of vinyls leaning against the wall. The couch was a hand-me-down, and the coffee table was scarred with old burns from forgotten mugs. But it was ours. And after everything we'd been through, that made it perfect.

Laken appeared behind me, wrapping his arms around my waist and resting his chin on my shoulder. "You're officially moved in," he murmured, his voice low and content.

I smiled, leaning back into him. "Feels weird. Good, but weird."

He chuckled. "Your dad gave me one of his famous silent nods this morning when I picked up the last box. Didn't say much."

I sighed, not surprised. "He's still not thrilled. He wanted me to stay at home longer."

Laken squeezed me a little tighter. "He'll come around."

I nodded, then turned in his arms to look up at him. "He just misses her. He misses us. But this..." I glanced around the room. "This is where I want to be."

He kissed my forehead softly. "Then this is where I'll make sure you feel safe."

A serene silence enveloped us—no ominous curse looming overhead, no forest whispering secrets to us in hushed tones—just an overwhelming sense of tranquility. Yet, amidst this newfound calm, I often found myself drawn to the small desk drawer where I had tucked away the abandoned sensor and camera chip. We hadn't unlocked their mysteries yet. Wesley was still deep into his research, poring over data and algorithms, determined to crack the code of what we had captured. Despite their inconspicuousness, they had not slipped from our minds.

Questions lingered like shadows. Strange readings flickered sporadically on Wesley's charts, and there were echoes in the data we couldn't quite comprehend. Despite the enigma, there was a comforting realization that we had time now. Time to heal our wounds, time to embrace the bonds we had forged through the trials we faced, and indeed, time to resume our search for answers.

In the quiet hours of the night, when the world outside my apartment hushed into a tranquil stillness, I often reflected on my friends and the paths they had chosen after everything unraveled. Wesley had returned to Georgia not long after the dust settled, citing a strong need for space to process everything, to breathe, and, perhaps, to rest his weary mind. He had promised that he was merely a phone call away and kept that promise with unwavering resolve. Every strange reading I sent his way, every late-night theory I entertained, drew an immediate response. His commitment to our shared experiences shone brightly through the darkness.

Ashten had slipped back to Texas. Her departure was quiet, marked only by a tearful hug and a whispered insistence of "no more spooky shit." Although she still reached out, sending memes that made me laugh, sharing outfit selfies that showcased her evolving style, and delivering her signature sarcastic commentary on the absurdity of life, she never spoke of Oak Hollow. That chapter felt permanently closed; perhaps it was best left untouched.

Tora had stayed close for a while, but eventually she had her fill of chasing the unknown. "The only kind of science I'm interested in now is the culinary variety," she had said, a smile gracing her face that bespoke her newfound joy. Last I heard, she was immersed in a culinary apprenticeship under a talented chef, running a vibrant pop-up restaurant in Asheville. With each care package she sent, filled with handwritten recipes and meticulously labeled spice blends, I could feel her warmth and creativity enveloping me, even from afar.

Each of us carried the weight of our experiences with us, no matter how we chose to address them. I was no exception. But in the depths of my heart, I also held something else: a flickering hope. There was a deep-seated hunger for the truth that vibrated in harmony with my very being. I was not finished with Oak Hollow. Not by a long shot.

The evening unfolded quietly, while the tantalizing scent of dinner lingered in the air, and remnants of a comforting meal wafted from the kitchen. I found myself absorbed in jotting down notes in the margins of one of my mother's old field journals, the pages yellowed with time, each word echoing her passion for exploration and discovery, when suddenly the front door swung open with a force that shattered the calm.

Laken burst into the room, breathless, his keys still dangling from his hand. "Did you hear?"

I lifted my gaze, the comforting warmth of the moment replaced by a prickling tension. "Hear what?"

He ran a hand through his tousled hair, his eyes wide and filled with a mix of anxiety and excitement. "Another hiker. Near Oak Hollow. They found him this morning, alive but distorted. The poor guy claims he was only gone for a few hours but was missing for three days."

I stared at him, my heart pounding violently in my chest; the familiar grip of dread coiled tightly around my bones. I whispered what I knew to be the only immutable truth that had ever mattered to me.

"The forest never forgets. It waits."

With urgency igniting my every move, I stood up abruptly, snatching my worn backpack from the corner, the familiar weight of it settling comfortably on my shoulder. My boots, already positioned by the door, awaited me.

Laken needed no further invitation. He grabbed his flashlight and fell in step beside me, unwavering in his commitment. I glanced over my shoulder, my eyes hardened with a quiet resolve.

"We've got work to do."

ABOUT THE AUTHOR

Brandy Nacole is a writer of paranormal suspense and YA mystery. She's penned the bestselling novels *Deep in the Hollow, The Shadow World Trilogy,* and *I Will Bury You*.

She loves keeping readers on the edge of their seats as that's where she likes to stay. Her favorite pastimes are reading, writing, exploring the world, and spending as much time with her husband, kids, and fur babies as possible. If Brandy can't be found, it's okay, she's not lost. She's frolicking in the woods somewhere and will return for tacos eventually.

You can also find her on:
Amazon: amzn.to/38AP5HO
Instagram: www.instagram.com/brandy_nacole
Facebook: www.facebook.com/authorbrandynacole
Goodreads: www.goodreads.com/BrandyNacole

Other Books by Brandy

The Shadow World Trilogy:
Uniquely Unwelcome (Book 1)
Blood Burdens (Book 2)
Sacrifice: A New Dawn (Book 3)

The Chindi Series:
Deep in the Hollow (Book 1)
Buried in the Bayou (Book 2)
Whispers in the Lake (Book 3)
Secrets in the Valley (Book 4)

Murder Is A Debate
Murder Is A Game

I Will Bury You (A YA Psychological Thriller)

Don't Lie to Me (A YA Psychological Thriller)

Spiritual Discord Series:
Broken Faith (Book 1)
Raging Storm (Book 2)
Darkest Reaches (Book 3)
Breath of Life: Part 1 (Book 4)

Fade Unto Darkness: An All Hallows' Eve Origin Story

Made in the USA
Columbia, SC
22 June 2025

59694068R00117